Confessions OF A So-called Middle Child

Confessions of a So-called Middle Child

by Maria T. Lennon

HARPER

An Imprint of HarperCollins Publishers

Library of Congress Cataloging-in-Publication Data
Lennon, M. T. (Maria T.)
    Confessions of a so-called middle child / by Maria T. Lennon — First edition.
        pages   cm
    Summary: Charlie C. Cooper, reformed bully, gifted hacker, and middle child
wants to make "cool" friends at her new school in Los Angeles, but her psychologist
tasks her with becoming friends with the school's "biggest loser."
    ISBN 978-0-06-212690-0 (hardback)
    [1. Middle-born children—Fiction. 2. Friendship—Fiction. 3. Popularity—
Fiction. 4. Bullies—Fiction. 5. Middle schools—Fiction. 6. Schools—Fiction.
7. Family life—California—Fiction. 8. Los Angeles (Calif.)—Fiction.] I. Title.
PZ7.L53935Con 2013   2013021365
[Fic]—dc23   CIP
                                                                              AC

Typography by Michelle Gengaro-Kokmen
13 14 15 16 17   CG/RRDH   10 9 8 7 6 5 4 3 2 1

First Edition

Dedicated to all the Charlies out there and the people who love them

Confessions OF A So-called Middle Child

Dead Girl Walking

9:00 a.m. What twelve-year-old kid is forced to spend her last day of summer vacation *reading books* in her room?

Charlie C. Cooper, that's who.

Yep, this summer I'm pretty sure I've spent more time in my room than a prisoner does in his cell.

After the hour mark, I got off my bed. Quietly, I turned the door handle all the way and put one foot out of my room, just to get a sense of what kind of trouble I was in.

But Mom has the ears of a panther, a really mean, old panther. She heard the click before I could even breathe. "Get back in there." She said it like she was right there when she was all the way downstairs—see what I mean?

"But Mom." I grabbed my hair and ripped. "Please, I beg of you, it's the last day of summer."

"Read the book." She said it without even thinking about

1

it. I told you she was mean. I wanted to die. My life was so not fair.

Tell me, how long can a child be punished for something she did months ago?

"Close that door, Charlie." Mom yelled from the bottom of the stairs.

Oh, but I smelled pumpkin bread that was gonna be gone by the time I broke out of here. "Child cruelty!" I shouted.

"Charlie C. Cooper!"

I slammed the door as fast as I could to avoid the dreaded stomp of her Birkenstock sandals. Talk about arrestable offenses—she had so many pairs of them, her closet just gave me the creeps, all those Birkenstocks. What's wrong with a pair of Manolos or a splash of Louboutin?

"Three more hours, Charlie." Dad sounded happy. Can you believe it? Probably because he was enjoying some of that bread I could smell but would never eat.

I was going to die in this room, I could feel it happening, like one of those nasty, hairy, old icemen with frozen beards and unibrows, buried under the pile of stinkin' books she forced me to read from eight until noon every day for the entire summer. Yep, while my little brother, Felix, and moody teenage sister, Penelope, with armpit hair you could braid, were out frolicking around our new digs at the Houdini Estate in the Hollywood Hills, I was locked in my room reading. And you know what? The whole reason we were even here was because of me. Yep, me. We were forced to move here because of something I did.

Truth is, I did something really bad. And I mean really, really bad. Bad enough to get expelled for. Bad enough to have to move cities for. Bad enough to have to read books the entire summer for. *But*, and I want to be super clear on this, I was the victim. And if you don't believe me, you will by the end of these confessions.

I was the one who'd been wronged. I was the one who'd been dumped, dropped, and practically left for dead when that new girl, Ashley Stronza, came to my school from stuck-up old London with her fancy accent and her off-the-rack Topshop wardrobe and stole my best friend in the world, Roxy.

So I had to get rid of Ashley. Send her back to England. That's all I was trying to do. I'd read about this kid who as a prank put laxatives in the lunch food at some school in Des Moines and got kicked out. Easy, right? And pretty dang harmless too. Plus we were in Malibu, where people pay big money to have this kinda stuff done to them every day.

Before you make any rash judgments about me, let me repeat:

1. It was not my idea.
2. Cleansing is healthy.
3. The laxatives were organic.
4. We lived in Malibu.

And it took months of dedication and hard work to collect dozens of laxatives from grown-ups' bathrooms. It was seriously gross.

See, I had to crush 'em all up, pour them into Ashley's super dumb Union Jack water bottle. Then I had to wait until all the kindergartners had eaten, which was majorly nerve-racking. See, they eat at 11:30, and I so did not need a whole bunch of sick kindergartners on my conscience. When the coast was clear, I snuck into the cafeteria, sprinkled the stuff all over the food. Then I left her bottle where they could find it and sat back in the sunlight to dream of a better life without Ashley in it.

But the world was against me, yet again.

See, it turned out they had a performance I didn't know about, so their lunchtime got bumped up and they were eating with the rest of us. When they came into the cafeteria, with their faces painted like dumb farm animals, ready to dive in, I nearly had a heart attack. Don't get me wrong, I'm not nice or anything. It's just that I had nothing against them, all right?

I tried to stop 'em. I screamed, yelled, but they wouldn't listen, being dumb little kids and all. They spooned it onto their plates and gobbled up all those laxatives. I couldn't watch it, thinking about what was about to transpire in their stomachs. Then the rest of the school came in, but it was too late. So I confessed and paid the price.

It wasn't pretty. The cops came. The school kicked me out, and I had to see a shrink all summer long. But the one cool thing out of all of this mess was that my dad found a job rebuilding the huge, the awesome Houdini mansion, as in home of Harry

Houdini, the greatest magician who ever lived.

I went to the window, opened it. "I'll die reading. Just kill me now, why don't you?"

"Reading won't kill you, Charlie," Mom called up from the kitchen.

"Oh, yes it will. Haven't you ever heard of the disease where the synapses in your brain explode due to concentrated eye movement, otherwise known as reading?"

"Read. Now!"

For some reason she didn't sound too worried, so I added some medical facts. "Yeah, it's true. Blood pours into your eyes, so they get like big fishbowls with your pupils just swimming around. It was on TV, I swear."

"You've got just a few hours to go," repeated mean Mom.

"Or that thing where your head just explodes from that life-threatening eye pressure brought on by staring at those lines, those words, all those terrible words?" I was feeling sick at the thought of it. "It's getting blurry, Mom."

"And after you finish your reading, I want to see your life plan."

"Life plan?" Yikes. What was I, like fifty? Who plans, any-way? Why plan when everything changes?

She turned on the water to wash the dishes. In the back-ground I could hear that spoiled lucky brat Felix watching cartoons. "A plan for how you'll be a productive part of this family, Charlie," she called up. "No more talking, all right?"

I fell back on my bed and looked at the pile of books I'd read so far:

1. *Love Thine Enemy, Love Thyself.* Can you believe that language? THINE? I mean, seriously? Yuck. That thing was written back in the days when older sisters enslaved their younger ones. When people put tar on wounds and bled you when you got the sniffles. I skimmed that book big-time.

2. *Anger: It's Natural.* Better than natural. It's essential, like oxygen. Without anger, who would I be?

3. *Embrace Your Inner Middle Child.* Written by my very own shrink, this book could end life on this planet, because most people would prefer killing themselves instead of turning another page. Myself included.

4. *How Sugar Feeds into Anger.* My conclusion after spending two brain-numbing weeks on this: Thank God my anger had some decent food, right?

5. *Alert: Do You Have a Middle Child Living in Your Home?* This was the final book in the series of punishments. I'd put it off because of the fact that it was more than five hundred pages. I didn't even look at it until this morning when they forced me to.

I picked it up with total disgust, cracked it open with dread, when what did I see? *Pictures!* I flipped the pages and was thrilled to see more and more pictures of this kid with a really mean and seriously creepy look on her face. On closer inspection I saw a sharp knife in her hands, which she was hiding behind her back. Wow, this kid was cool. Kinda like that weird girl in *Orphan* with those freaky black teeth.

So I propped up my pillows, and faster than you could say "Charlie Cooper will be bigger than Steve Jobs," I read ten pages just like that. I don't think I'd ever really read more than five pages without brain pain. But this, this was like reading a diary. My diary. This kid with the cute little blond ponytails was me.

The Middle Child, Me, Girl with Knife usually had an older sister who was "better" at just about everything—except eating. Which is way true in my case. Penelope and Felix don't like to eat. How weird is that? Doesn't that just show you that they might not be human after all?

I got out my black reading glasses—lenses poked out—that I got from the *Jaws 3D* movie I saw before my grounding began, and I got the strangest feeling *ever*. I actually liked the book. For the first time since my reading sentence began and my mom made me read books about what makes a middle child tick, this book was the first one that seemed to be talking straight to me. It made me feel less like a freak, because when you have an older sister who's good at everything and you're, well, not, you have to act like you don't care. I was good at acting like I didn't care, but let me tell you a little secret: I did. I cared a lot.

At noon the warden (aka my mom) came and let me out

for lunch. I ran down the stairs kissing each and every bloody haunted hologram portrait that hung along the staircase. I've come to think of them as my best friends, you know, seeing as how I have no friends.

There's Josie, who looked so pretty when you passed her on the left, but man, oh man, when you saw her from the right, she was headless and dripping blood. And Frank, her husband, who wore a tight white collar, like a boring banker, but then when you caught the hologram in the right light, bingo! His brains were splattered like raindrops. I gave him the biggest kiss of all. "Good afternoon, my peeps!" I announced at the bottom of the stairs to Penelope (reading) and Felix (playing with his thing-a-ling), and dived into the grilled cheese and the tomato soup Mom had made. "That was delicious."

I jumped up, looked around. "Hey, where's Dad?" I had some serious exploring to do. It was the last day of summer and still Dad and I had not gotten any closer to finding Houdini's secret tunnels, lost since 1936. Legend had it that they held treasures and potentially lucrative secrets beyond imagination. I had to unlock them.

Mom put my dishes in the dishwasher, picked up her purse, and said, "You ready to go?"

"Go where?" I looked at her. Images of back-to-school shopping floated through my mind, maybe a little Johnny Rockets double-cheese burger and a movie at the Grove. The tunnels could wait. I zipped up my super sleek black leather boots and called over to Pen and Felix, who, unlike yours truly, were allowed to watch TV every day of the entire summer, "Come on, you guys, we're leaving!"

But Mom shook her head. "This is just for you, Charlie."

Halt. Red alert. I stopped. It was never good to be singled out, trust me. "Just me?"

Mom picked up her keys. "Yes, just you, Charlie."

Oh, crap. She took me by the arm, and we went out into the horrible sunlight. Did I mention I hate the sun?

Here's Hoping—
My Very Last Trip
to the Shrink

Sadly, of course I knew where we were going. But as I am a glass-half-full type of gal, I saw this as the very likely *end* of my mental-health plan.

We headed south down the hill, took a right onto Sunset Boulevard, and passed the old guy waving his flag. He had his dog under his picnic chair, a yummy-looking iced Starbucks coffee drink, and a boom box. He was trying to get to San Francisco.

You know, I kinda envied that dude. Not only was he was in control of his destiny, he was wearing a seriously cool set of cowboy boots.

We got to the big block of buildings, scary buildings that smelled like white coats, alcohol, and really long needles. Man, did I hate these places. I could smell 'em a mile away.

Over the last three months, they'd been forcing me to come

here once a week to discuss my feelings. I mean, how many feelings can a twelve-year-old girl have in a week? I had to make them up; I had to invent problems I didn't even have. But today, today was the end of summer, which had to mean the end of therapy! Hallelujah!

Mom knocked on the door, and it opened right away like Dr. Scales had nothing better to do. Let me warn you, the dude was ugly but in a friendly, old, grandpa, I-left-my-teeth-at-home sort of way. He wore his last remaining strands of hair in a comb-over and had huge teeth that made you think of Old Yeller. But he was one of the nicest dudes I've ever known. And he helped me, he did. Not that there was anything wrong with me *at all*, but I am a middle child, you know.

"Charlie." He opened the door wide. "Hello."

"Bam!" I pretended to kick him in the shins for old times' sake. When I first came, I was a completely different person. Put it this way: I was like the Hulk; now I'm more Bruce Banner.

He looked at my boots, my outfit. "Are you going as a Power Ranger this Halloween?"

"What!" How old did he think I was? Six? I was wearing a super cool leotard that happened to be yellow and white, a white skirt, and seriously swag black high-heel boots.

He laughed and tossed me a high five like he had swag. "I'm just messing with you, Charlie!"

"You're killing me, Doc." I collapsed into the deep sofa.

Now Dr. Scales scooted forward. "So your new school starts tomorrow, huh, Charlie? How do you feel?"

I looked at them both. The more I studied their faces, the weirder Mom and Doc Scales looked. The doc had hairs everywhere, and Mom, well, lines were forming on her face. I sure hoped I didn't look like that when I got older. Old age blows. Anyway, I gave them the thumbs-up and announced with as much enthusiasm as I could muster, "I feel excited, Doc. I feel *ready*."

"New school, new you." He opened my file, which he always had on his desk whenever we had our sessions. Sometimes he'd lean over and jot something down; sometimes he'd give me a glance, a nudge, just to scare the crap out of me. "I feel like you're ready; really, really ready."

I could barely speak. "I am, Doc, I so am!" Was this the moment I'd been longing for? The moment when he'd tell me I was done, that I'd never have to come here again and talk about my feelings?

He nodded like this was it. "You must be aware of your triggers."

"My triggers?" What the heck?

"Popular girls." He shook his head. "You're attracted to them, Charlie, because you crave acceptance. But your self-esteem"—he looked like a sad, old pound dog—"is low. So you get their attention by being bad."

Like I hadn't heard that before. "But not anymore. I've been so good this summer, it's sickening." I pointed to my mom, who was pretending to read. "Just ask my mom. Ask her."

She looked up. "It's true."

"And I've lost a few pounds"—I sucked it in—"or haven't you noticed?"

"All right," he said, smiling, "I respect that. Let's talk about your last school, Charlie."

Here we go again. "I've already talked about it until there's nothing left to talk about, Doc. I put some laxatives in the cafeteria food. The school had a massive cleanse, could have gone on that show *The Biggest Loser*." I leaned back and waited for him to laugh. He didn't.

Mom stomped her feet on the floor. "Charlie, stop with the sarcasm!"

"All right, all right! I'm sorry. It was a mistake, I temporarily lost my mind, okay?" But really, you wanna know the truth? It was really Ashley's fault. If she hadn't moved here and set her sights on Roxy, my best—and, okay, fine—my only friend, and made a point of ditching me like a piece of you know what, *none* of this, and I repeat, none of this would have ever happened. But of course I could never say that to Dr. Scales, or he'd make me come twice a week.

TRUE FACT: Whenever I can't sleep, I just dream of Ashley getting run over by the biggest truck you've ever seen. Works like a charm every time.

"I'm going to get a coffee." Mom got up, as usual. See, when you're a kid seeing a shrink, your mom or dad hang out for a few minutes and make small talk like it's a voluntary thing, like it's *fun* or something. Then they take off fast. "I'll see you in an hour."

As soon as the door closed, Doc Scales went back to reading from my file. Crap! That file was thick. "But"—he turned the page—"you ended up letting yourself get caught, because you didn't want the kindergartners getting sick. Compassion, Charlie, the other side of the bully."

"For the last time, I'm no bully." I sat up straight. That word just pissed me off. "Have you ever seen bullies, Doc? Do they look like this?" I pointed to my gorgeous hair, my incredible leggings, my smile. "No, they don't. They look like huge monsters who wear cutoff denim shorts and vests, all right?"

"I was going to say, Children who are bullied often show remarkable compassion." He paused like it hadn't sunk in already. "Like you did; you got caught because you were compassionate."

I looked away. My God, did we have to rehash this whole thing? "A moment of weakness."

"They clapped when you were forced to leave?" He looked at me with those deep eyes like he was testing me to see whether I was going to flip out. "How did that make you feel?"

"Uh, not great, Doc," I said easily, but the truth was, the thought of it still made me sweat. I could still remember

Ashley Stronza's first day. She wore black lipstick, had a fake nose piercing, and swore she played spin the bottle. I recognized her for the fraud she was. But no one else did. To put it mildly, her arrival at the end of fifth grade at Malibu Charter ruined everything.

Dr. Scales nodded and scanned the notes again. He kept flipping them and flipping them. Jeez, how many pages did he have on me? "At home you're the middle child. Your fourteen-year-old sister excels academically, has a million causes she fights for. Your seven-year-old brother—" Doc must have had a picture in that file, because his face got all soft and sappy when he said, "Boy, he really could be in one of those Gap ads, couldn't he?"

"You're killing me, Doc."

"My point is, Charlie, at home you've made your mark by being bad. That's how you've always gotten attention."

"Yeah, well, as you know, the other spots were taken." I bit my nail.

"But that puts you in a very unique position," he stated. "You know more than anyone what it feels like to be left behind, to be treated like yesterday's news. Ditched, dodged, abandoned at the lunch tables—"

"All right, all right!" Just the memory of it was making me get all hot.

"You've read my book, *Embrace Your Inner Middle Child*?"

I rolled my eyes. "Took me half of July."

"So you recall the second-to-last chapter, 'The Mark of the Middle'?"

Nope, I blocked it out. I blocked all of it out. You see, most of the time when I'm "reading," my eyes are moving over the pages, but my mind is thinking about hacking computer codes and runway fashion. Baby, that's what makes my life worth living.

"You carry with you the mark of the middle child, and people know it." He pointed at my heart. "They sense it. Kids most of all."

"So what are you saying?"

"I'm saying stay away from the popular girls. Do not dive in and search out the best-dressed, most beautiful girls. Slow down; wait."

"No worries, I got it," I said. "I can wait." In fact, I wanted to wait. Nope, no more rush, rush, rush for me. But seriously, now I had to go. "Thanks for everything, Doc." I got up, clapped. "I'm excited, Doc. This is going to be great—a fresh start where no one knows my name. I will not blow this. I'll never forget you." I was laying it on thick because I was just about to walk out that door and *never*, and I mean *never*, turn back.

Scales pointed to the chair. "Not done." He made me sit back down and then, as adults always do, he kept going on and on, covering *no* new ground. "There's something you must do on your first day."

"Sure, fine." I tapped my foot anxiously.

"If you can complete this task"—he gave me the hairy-eyebrow wiggle—"you won't have to come here anymore."

"Done." I pounced.

"Your task is"—his eyes popped out, just like a French bulldog, his crooked fingers were all entwined, he leaned so close I could smell his hair—"to find the most bullied girl in your class and be her friend. Yes, Charlie, befriend her." He let out a deep breath.

"What?" I glared. "Excuse me? Come again? *Sprechen sie Deutsch? Parlez-vous français?* Speak English?"

He narrowed his eyes. You could barely see them under all that hair. "I think you heard me."

"But, but that's like the kiss of death, Doc. I'll be ruined, ruined before I even begin. Do you know the work I've done this summer? The outfits I've put together? I'm ready to go, Doc, to have a fresh start, and there's no way on this earth I can start my new life by hanging out with the lowest of the low."

Dr. Scales came around from his desk and lifted my chin. "I know you think I'm doing you a great disservice, but believe me when I tell you I want you to succeed, Ms. Charlie Cooper, I want you to succeed more than you can ever know. But you must stand on your own two feet and succeed as a human being first."

I could barely get up, such was my despair. "I don't want to be a human being! I just want to have friends, Doc, and lots of them." I walked to the door. What was left to say? Oh, there was one thing left. "You know what it's like being the only one *not* getting the evite, Doc? It's horrible. It's like a knife in the heart over and over. And if I do what you ask, I'll be putting the knife in my own heart!"

"Does your sister have lots and lots of friends?"

I looked away. He knew the answer.

"It's because she doesn't care about popularity, Charlie. She cares about bigger things, more important things. You make your mark by being kind to those no one is kind to, and everyone will want to be friends with you."

Blah, blah, blah—just kill me now.

He touched my arm. "Trust me."

"Blackmailer." I closed my eyes. I felt deflated and horrible. Not only was this *not* my last session, he was basically branding me a total *loser* before I even had a chance to wow everyone with my fashion sense, my wit, my undeniable charm.

"Time's up." He got up, walked to the door. "By next week I'm sure you'll have found the girl whose life you'll change."

"And what if there isn't one, huh?" I felt one last surge of hope. "What if they're all like happy little Smurfs, huh? What if it's a bully-free school, what then, Doc?"

"I've never known one." He smiled. "And I'll trust you to be honest," he said. "Or the sessions will continue until you are honest, Charlie."

I wanted to kick him in the shins more than I wanted to breathe. "Great."

Mom was filling a cup with water from the water cooler when I came through. She looked up, hopeful. "So how'd it go?"

I felt like puking. "Horrible. I'm his slave, his slave for life."

Mom looked at Scales. "Not done?"

"Not quite," he said softly. "See you next week, Charlie." Then he closed the door before I could give him a dirty look.

On the drive home, Mom reached over and touched my knee. "Hey, Charlie, what happened in there? You seem really upset."

I looked out the window, watching all the grown-ups go by and wishing I could do what I wanted, just like them. "He's blackmailing me."

Mom laughed. "What?"

"He's telling me that I have to pretend to befriend the biggest loser in my class."

Mom thought long and hard and then said, "Huh."

"Huh?" I wanted to explode. "Is that all you can say?"

"Huh, as in: There's probably a good reason why he's doing it." She checked the mirror and tried to merge into the lane going up into the canyons, but no one would let us in. "Jeez, these jerks won't let me merge."

"It's called revenge." He was trying to make my life miserable, that's what he was doing.

Mom rolled down the window on the old Volvo with peeling Clinton-Gore stickers and yelled, "Where's the love, man? Show me some love." The cars stopped. I tried to hide under the seat so no one would see me. Mom waved like she wasn't totally embarrassing me, thankful and with a renewed sense of love for all mankind. "Dr. Scales cares about you. I think you need to trust him."

"He's mean, and I hate him."

We chugged up the canyon. Mom said, "He's giving you the responsibility of standing for something. He's making you a better person, Charlie, even if you don't want to be."

"Oh my God! What don't I stand for? I stand for fashion, Mom. And cracking rockin' computer software. I stand for—"

"You need to stand for something right. He's helping you down a new path; you have to go down it and see for yourself what it brings."

"I know what it's going to bring." The anger was coming back—why weren't these old people listening to me? "It's going to turn me into an untouchable, like Jai told me they have in India, Mom, that's what it's gonna do, and then I'll be right back in the same place I was when I left Malibu. Hated. Laughed at. Left out. It sucks, Mom." I started to cry, so I hid my face. The last thing I wanted was for her to give me one of those sad looks. I did not want consolation; I wanted her to call it off.

"I'm sorry." Her voice cracked. "It's been so hard for you, Charlie, and it kills me to see you like this."

I grabbed my knees and hugged them hard to my chest. "Then tell him no."

"I can't."

"Why? Why can't you? Can't you see that it's going to ruin my chances, and you always say there aren't many fresh starts in life, right, Mom?"

Mom pulled off to the right and put her hand on my knee. "I can't because I think he might be right." We drove up the dusty, old road that led through the seriously haunted-looking wrought-iron gates of the Houdini Estate. As soon as she pulled up to the gatekeeper's house, I threw the door open and yelled, "I hate you, Mom!" I ran into the kitchen and saw Felix doodling and, of course, my sister reading again.

Pen looked up. "What happened?"

I could see that thrill in her eyes. She always had it when she thought I was in trouble. I went right up to her, got so close I could bite her. "It's all because of you." Then I ripped the book out of her hands and threw it across the floor.

Sadly, Mom was standing right there. "Just go cool off in your room, Charlie."

"Love to." I ran up the creaky, old stairs and pushed open the red door to our room. Yeah, that's right. *Our* room. We're forced to share a room, which is, I believe, a crime against humanity under international law. I hit the switch for the butterfly lights Mom had woven through the loft. The windows were tall and overlooked the gardens and the main street, Laurel Canyon Boulevard. I cracked one open. A gust of air lifted the linen curtain, and suddenly I felt like I wasn't alone in this horrible life of mine.

On my wall were the dudes who had gotten me through my

21

summer of hell and were helping me out right now, big-time:

First and foremost, Nelson Mandela. If he could survive twenty-seven years behind bars, and forgive his enemies for their wrongs, so could I, right?

Steve Jobs. Because like him, I wished the world was populated with little Macs and iPads instead of real, feeling, pain-in-the-neck people.

Since I'd logged on early that morning, I had thirty-five Skype attempts from Jai, my tech-equal main squeeze in Mumbai. I was just about to log on and wake up my Indian brother-in-arms when Mom called from downstairs, "Charlie, do you want pizza or mac and cheese for dinner?"

I smiled. Those were code words for "I'm sorry," "I love you," and "Please come down and be a part of our family," because I could eat mac and cheese for breakfast, lunch, and dinner. I got up and cracked open the door. "It's not home-made, right?"

"Velveeta all the way."

"Yes!" I opened the door and ran to the top of the stairs. "Two boxes?"

"One." She looked up at me. "The pediatrician says you shouldn't eat two helpings, remember?"

I rolled my eyes. "Give me a break, will ya?"

"Come and help your sister set the table."

I closed my laptop. Velveeta took precedence over all else; Jai would have to wait. I ran down the stairs, and my nose became alive with the smell of all that wondrous fake cheese. I went to work tossing out the place mats, the bowls, forks, and cups.

I was just singing along, not complaining, when Pen came over, picked my beloved Velveeta box out of the trash, and started reading. I ignored her. She gasped. Mom turned. "What?"

"Did you know there's no actual cheese in this stuff, and there's twelve grams of fat per serving?" She cringed. "Jeez, that sure is a lot of fat."

I wanted to slap her. But I didn't. See, I was learning.

First Day of the New Me

The next morning, while it was still dark and everyone was spewing their nasty morning breath into the air, I jumped out of bed in need of spiritual guidance, no joke. I pulled my bedazzled robe off the hook, slipped into my fuzzy-dice slippers, and tiptoed down the stairs, kissing the portraits of my friends. Outside, the sun was cutting through the heavy mist. A bunch of wild rabbits ran across the yard, disappearing up the mountain.

Five whole acres of freedom in the Hollywood Hills! Poor Houdini; he wanted to live here forever, but the man who could escape from a box submerged in water while handcuffed, who could stand to be buried alive in a box of sand for one hour and thirty minutes, could not escape a burst appendix. Life can really suck sometimes.

I ran up the hill, and in the middle of the tall, wild grasses, I found my new favorite place to hang out—right under the statue of Mr. Houdini himself. I had learned so much from this man over the summer, more than from any of those dumb books Mom made me read. This was a man who knew how to reinvent himself, which was all I wanted to do.

I mean, seriously, the man did not stop changing his name until he got it just right—first it was Erik Weisz of Hungary. Then Erich Weiss. Finally, it must have hit him that drama matters. So he went with Mr. Harry Houdini of Appleton, Wisconsin.

And he kept on reinventing along the way. Stage-show performer, magician, Hollywood star, ghost. He was smart, that Harry Houdini. He turned himself into something special, something that broke the mold, *and* did it without selling his soul. People came from all over, begging and bribing him to reunite them with the dead, and he turned them down flat. Anyway, that's why they hired my dad to rebuild the whole place and turn it into a museum. I just wished Houdini was a little better-looking.

I'd closed my eyes, trying to channel a little of his confidence, when Mom called out, "Charlie! Baby, where are you?"

I got up and waved to her. "Coming!"

"You'd better get dressed; you don't want to be late on your first day!" She smiled at me like she really loved me, and, you know what, I really loved her too. I ran down the grassy hill

I had come to know so well over my grounded summer, went into the house and up the stairs, and opened my humble closet. I had my outfit already picked. I was ready.

For my first day of school, I had carefully chosen my absolute favorite pair of faux snakeskin leggings. I'd had them since I was eight, so they were a little tight, but who cares, right? Oh, did I tell you that I gained more weight in my sixth-grade year than in my entire life? Seeing Ashley in those super trendy drainpipe jeans every day, giggling up and down with Roxy in *matching* drainpipes, well, it made me want to stick my head in the fridge for the rest of my life.

Anyway, that was then. Now, for the first day, I had on a pink tutu, a black Guns N' Roses T-shirt, and a white tank top, and for the details—it's all in the details—cowboy boots and gloves without fingers. Penelope passed by the bathroom door and covered her face. In a heartbeat I knew what she felt. Envy. It wasn't easy having a fashion icon in the house. I waved to Dad, and for no apparent reason he ran out the door. Late for work, I guess.

When Mom walked in, she looked pretty startled. "What on earth are you wearing?"

I gave her my stare of death. "There's no way you can make me take it off."

TRUE FACT: You have to stand firm when it comes to fashion. Just ask Coco. And if you don't know who that is, you shouldn't even be reading this.

"It's too tight now." She squeezed her eyes shut. "They'll laugh, baby."

Laughing! Please, you think I care? "All great designers have to suffer, Mom; that's just the way it goes."

She gave me one of those heavy looks. "Did you at least brush your teeth?"

"Of course." Are you kidding me? Not brushing your teeth is for Losers, capital L. I grabbed a piece of bacon, looked out over the hills, and nibbled.

Pen came running down the stairs in an outfit I could only describe as "Anne Frank." It was a dark, sad *jumpsuit*—enough said, right? She even had her long, mousy, blond hair in two braids, her skin all pale from the Model UN summer camp she went to. Poor Pen. Put it this way—you could see her mustache from across the street. Flies could land on her leg hair. It was that bad. In the old days, I'd just let her go out like that, but now that I was different, I had to offer my assistance. "Uh, Pen, that jumpsuit"—how to put this without sounding mean—"I wouldn't."

"It's cute," Mom said. "Jumpsuits are in."

"Yeah." I gobbled up the bacon. "In North Korea."

"Charlie!" Mom warned. She held the evil eye steady. "Enough."

"I was just trying to help." I poured more juice. "Seriously, I don't want people to get the wrong impression of her."

Pen covered her face. "Oh my God, please, make it stop!"

Dad, who had come back for another cup of coffee, nudged Pen's arms. "Come on, Pen, lighten up. She's just looking out for you. Maybe jumpsuits aren't in this year, you know, Charlie's hip to these things—she reads *Vogue*." He said it like he thought it was funny. It wasn't. Fashion is serious stuff. Ever see Anna Wintour smile? I didn't think so.

Pen dropped her uneaten breakfast in the sink. The dishes banged. She glared at me. "You have so not changed."

"I have, I swear!" Seriously? How could they doubt me? "I promised, remember, I'm going to be nice."

"But you can't. It's biologically impossible for you to be kind," Pen said. "It's not even eight in the morning, and you've already totally made me feel like crap." When the kitchen light flashed off her braces, she actually looked kinda scary, but I said nothing. "You're just mean."

"I am so not mean." No matter how hard I tried, I couldn't take my eyes off her braces.

"Sometimes you are, Charlie. Sorry," Felix totally interrupted.

My watch beeped. I took a deep breath. "Well, this has been fun with a capital F, but it's time to go to school." I picked up my super cool black-on-black faux snakeskin backpack and was about to walk out the door when Mom pulled me back in and gave me that look of motherly concern.

Pen stormed past me, hitting me with her backpack. "Forget it, Mom. She's incapable."

"I was trying to help, I swear."

"I know." Mom stared me down. "Just find the girl and be nice to her. Let that be your first act. Let that define you before all else."

Dad came over and kissed me on the forehead. "You have the power to change, Charlie."

"Oh, please." Pen snorted like she was Kim Jong #2.

"You sure you still want to walk? I'd love to drive you," Mom asked us again, even though we'd gone over it the night before.

"Yep, we want to walk," Pen said. "I want to be way out in the front, not near *her*." She opened the door, about to take off.

"Nope." Dad stopped her. "You will walk together, you hear me? You may dislike each other sometimes, but you will be brother and sisters to each other until the day you die. So deal with it."

Pen could hold a grudge forever, but not me; I got over them so fast, I sometimes forgot I even had them.

Mom was getting all teary. "We'll be right here when you get back. Have a wonderful day." They stood at the door and watched the three of us walk to the crosswalk and wait for the light to change and begin what would become our morning journey under the canopy of low and twisted sycamore trees, up Lookout Mountain Road all the way to Happy Canyon School. It seemed to take minutes because there were so many cool houses to check out.

Like the old log cabin off to my right, tucked under giant trees and surrounded by giant boulders. Hot springs bubbled between the rocks and into a pool. You could smell it too. P-U. The gate was open. I couldn't wait to go in.

Apparently Pen was not a lover of nature, because she turned around and yelled at me. "Hurry up, Charlie!"

Happy Canyon School was just after the small stoplight on the left. The yard was already full of kids in their new duds, shooting basketballs, playing handball, or tossing footballs around. Ms. Genius/Hairy Dork eyed them the same way the Roman emperors did the slaves in the Colosseum before they were about to be killed for their pleasure. Pen thought sports were for people with small brains. She was a major snob that way. But maybe she would change here too. Felix stopped and stared at the kids running like crazy, and I could tell he couldn't wait.

Pen was the first to walk through the double doors of Happy Canyon.

There was a greeter asking for names and grades. She looked stuck to the chair, like she'd been sitting and waiting all summer long.

She handed Pen a map and schedule, and Pen was on her way without a worry in the world. Me next.

"Charlie Cooper, seventh grade," I announced.

"Ah," she said, like she was surprised. "We just had another Cooper. Was that your sister?"

I winked. "She's the middle child; you know how they can be."

"Gotcha." She checked me off her list and handed me my map and classroom info.

This school was so different from my last one. For starters, no one was staring at me; no one was sizing me up, checking out my clothes, my watch, my tan. The moment I walked into the corridor, I could feel myself growing hopeful.

Who Would I Be Today?

Inside the school there was a circle with benches and trees and bright tiles with handprints on the walls. I sat and pulled out the map. The lower yard divided the high school from the elementary and middle schools. I was assigned to a room on the second floor above the upper yard, the class of one very serious-sounding Mr. Hugh Lawson. I took a deep breath, about to march up those stairs like fear was not part of my DNA, when I heard:

"Charlie?" Felix, backpack dragging, papers falling out of his hand, tears in his eyes. "Do you know where I'm supposed to go?"

Really? Now? Just as I was about to make my grand entrance?

"Charlie?" His voice croaked. "I wish I'd let Mom come. I thought I could go by myself, but I can't."

I turned and saw him. The slumped shoulders, the red nose. "No worries, kid. Your secret's safe with me. I'll help you find it."

I took his papers, picked up his pack, and checked for his room. My sense of direction was infallible. Within seconds I found it, a bungalow behind the kindergarten classrooms. "Come on, follow me," I said, and walked him up the ramp.

The classroom was already full of kids sitting at round tables. On the walls were ABC cards, and on the carpet a rocking chair. Man, was Felix lucky. I bent down and pointed to the nicest-looking teacher I ever saw. "Welcome to first grade. Enjoy the heck out of it, because it's all downhill after this."

"Thanks, Charlie." He took his backpack and hugged me. "You're really nice sometimes."

"Yeah, yeah, don't go spreading the word, all right?" I watched him walk in; the teacher put her arm around him; the kids waved. Man, growing up really sucked.

Felix looked at me one last time. "Bye, Charlie."

"See ya, kid." I left the land of milk and cookies and went into the jungle. I took the stairs like I knew each one by heart and made my way down the crowded hall, packed with kids who knew one another, my stomach now seriously flip-flopping. I hadn't felt like this since kindergarten, when I walked into that room and saw Roxy, the girl I knew I'd be best friends with for life. And we all know how that turned out, right?

Over the summer I did some groundbreaking research on

the best way to start seventh grade in a new school.

Act like you need *no one.*

Act like you've got hordes of friends in your native home.

An English accent is key but must sound real, or major backfire will occur.

I chose my seat carefully—third row from the front, to the left. I was a master at seat selection. The seat I chose said *I am not the teacher's pet, but I could be if I wanted to, because I am super smart.* But as soon as I saw the kind of kids coming through, I knew I was far from small-time Malibu. I'd made it to the big city. They fell in like actors onstage playing different parts, some Goth with black hair, lips, and nails; a couple of punks; a few hip-hop types. A dude with a blue Mohawk came in. Next was a kid sporting a white suit, hat, and tie, who I was pretty sure was a girl. There was a girl with a nose ring; kids speaking Russian, Korean, Farsi, Hindi. I leaned back and watched them all from my seat. I didn't want to believe it yet, but so far it looked like, here, it was going to be different than Malibu, where you either looked good in a bikini or you didn't. Here, maybe, just maybe, it was cool to be whoever you wanted to be.

But then *they* walked in, en masse, their long hair curled, their makeup shiny, their clothes straight out of the pages of magazines. And in spite of myself, I could feel the old tug, the pull, the cry from deep down in my heart. *I so wanted to be one of them.* They were the populars. I could tell them from a mile away, blindfolded. Smell them from their perfume, their makeup, their gum. These were the girls who did everything first—first to date, to kiss, to see a movie with a boy *without* their moms sitting behind them. They were the first to get boobs and to show them. They were the ones girls like me followed for a living. Then, like a pack of dogs, they stopped at my desk and did a quick stop-and-sniff.

"Hey," I said casually, barely looking.

They pushed past me like I hadn't said a word, like I wasn't even there, and headed to the very back of the classroom, where they sat like they were waiting to get their nails done. More people came in. Boys with upper-lip hair and small muscles grunted like they thought they should. Nerds walked fast and tight like they had red ants in their tight white briefs. And then came the ones who had dried toothpaste smeared over their lips and that dead look in their eyes that came from playing with their Legos all night long.

I took out my binder, pretended to write something super important, but really I was scared that there would be no one I would really like. No one I could see and *know* in my heart and soul that we could be friends. It's not something you can fake, either. You know; you just know. A few minutes later, two girls walked in. Their names: Trixie Chalice and Babette Suivre. And, dang it, you know what? I got that feeling.

Trixie had long, blondish-brown hair down to her waist. She was super skinny with freckles, big floppy ears, and a glint in her eyes. And let's not even talk about those incredibly cool knee-high Converse tennis shoes I would have given a kidney for, but Mom said they were too expensive, whatever that's supposed to mean. Her purse looked like liquid gold, and when she saw me, she gave me the look-over and I could tell she approved the fashion I was working. Babette, who followed her like a puppy, had curly hair to her shoulders but not cool curly hair, if you get my drift.

TRUE FACT: I am a graduate of Mumbai Online Beauty School.

I could tell that she was *the* follower, zero spark. All right, I'll admit it, my first thought was *I can get rid of that one.* But then the new me, the better me, quickly silenced that awful, mean voice, that small red devil on my shoulder. *Be nice to everyone,* countered my new-and-improved self.

Trixie walked straight up to me like she wanted to meet me. I smiled. "Hey."

She looked me over. "You're in my seat."

Stop. Freeze. Now, if this ever happens to you, *do not* give in. If you *do*, you lose all credibility. Watch and learn. I lifted my black glasses over my head and said, "Didn't see your name on it."

With a glint in her eye, she tapped the desk. "Look underneath."

I did a quick check, and much to my delight, I saw carved

into the seat in letters pointed like sharp daggers, all swaying V's in purple and red, she'd written, *Trixie Chalice's Butt Goes Here So Get Yours Outa Here ASAP.* I knew the style like the back of my hand. "You know Versuz?"

Her whole face lit up. "He's only the greatest graffiti artist in LA, Of course I know Versuz. He's a genius."

My mouth dropped open. So did hers. That's all it took.

"Did it on the last day of last year." She put her finger to her lips and smiled. "Name's Trixie." She nodded. "This here's Babs."

I looked at Babs and knew right away that she was lost without Trixie. "I'm Charlie."

Babs put her hand out—weird, right?—and squeezed mine hard, really, really hard. The message came through loud and clear. I was a threat. But I wasn't, because I was reformed. No way would I ever do to her what Ashley had done to me. I stood up. "Here, take your desk. It's yours." I could tell right away that Trix knew I was giving her the respect she deserved. She squeezed in, Babs next to her, and I, well, I was right in front of them.

The bell rang. I was pretending to look at my schedule when a kid named Bobby walked in, all sweaty. He had light brown skin and a blondish-brown Afro that stood a good two hands over his head. He was covered in cool leather necklaces and beaded bracelets. Our eyes met; he kinda smiled. "Cool shades," he said.

Trix tapped me on the shoulder, leaned in, and whispered, "He's got a girlfriend in high school. Don't waste your time."

"Good morning, my soon to be massively intelligent, creative, and kind seventh grade class!" Our teacher, Mr. Lawson, came in juggling two tall stacks of books, which tumbled down the moment he reached his desk. "Man, those are heavy!" He was wearing shorts and a white shirt, and I could tell right away that his arms and legs were way skinnier than mine. On his feet—were hairy Birkenstocks. Lucky for me, his legs were less hairy than Pen's.

"Morning, morning, class. Take your seats while I just make this place feel good and cozy." He closed the door, got down on the floor, and plugged in his table lamp for a little, soft glow. I checked out the class once more. So far, no total losers, which meant one thing: Good-bye, Dr. Scales. I sat back, breathed a heavy sigh of *relief.* I even began dreaming about my brand-new glamorous life when suddenly the door swung open and hit the wall. Marta Urloff stormed into the room.

My heart sank. *Sank.* She was a horror. You could see it from space. I wanted to cry; I felt the sting of tears in my eyes. If I did what Scales asked of me, I could kiss all possible interaction with humans at this school good-bye.

She looked like a homeless Disney princess. She had on dirty pink velour pants, a matching Disney jacket, socks, and blackened pink Crocs. Her pale grayish-blond hair was matted so high, it looked like she was wearing a wig.

Babette leaned forward, giggling. "She's our very reason for waking up every morning."

On top of it all, she looked mean, like a pit bull with messed-up teeth.

"People say she was raised by wolves," Trixie said, mesmerized.

"She's a Gypsy from Romania," Babette said. "My father tells me to be careful of Gypsies."

Trixie rolled her eyes. "Babs over here is French. Every homeless person is automatically a Gypsy."

Marta parked her battered Cinderella roller suitcase and took a front-row seat. She turned and looked straight into my eyes. I gotta admit, I felt sick. And it wasn't because her teeth were a shade of yellow I had only seen on buttered popcorn, or that her nails were long and filled with grime. Nope. It was because I recognized that if I did what I had to do to get off Dr. Scales's couch, she would be my lunch date for the rest of my days.

Mr. Lawson came out from behind his desk and surveyed the room. It was packed. I counted thirty-eight kids. "Welcome to seventh grade." He waved to Marta. "Now, I'd like you to meet someone special."

I looked away; I was so not ready for this.

Mr. Lawson held up a stick of deodorant. "Who knows what this is?" He looked around. No one said a word. "This is Mr. Deodorant. And why am I holding him up? Because you don't know this yet, but by seventh grade you guys *stink*, all of you." He walked down the rows, handing one out to each of us.

"Keep it here; use it daily. Your bodies are all changing in gross ways that we'll address at the end of the year in *sex education*."

Nervous giggles all around. He stopped right in front of my desk. Great. "Charlie Cooper?"

That's when Bobby looked down and said in the cutest voice ever, "Oh come on, man, she doesn't stink that bad. Give her a break."

I turned around to look at him, to give him my full attention. "Wow, impressive. You're seriously funny."

Mr. Lawson slapped my desk. I turned back around and came face-to-face with my teacher's hairy nostrils. "Class, meet Cooper."

Chairs scratched against the floor as everyone tried to get a good look at yours truly. I adjusted my thick, black glasses, pushed away my dark bangs, and waved weakly like a total dork. "Hey."

"Charlie"—he went back to his desk and took a seat— "tell us a little about yourself. Just the juicy stuff though." He grinned like he thought he was super funny. "We love the juicy stuff, not the boring stuff."

I surveyed the room. "Um, well, I'm from Malibu—"

Mr. Lawson interrupted. "Did you go to Malibu Charter or Malibu Elementary?"

"Yeah! Give it up for the BU." Trixie clapped. "I know a whole bunch of people from there. I surf with them." She looked right at me, scooted closer. "Come on, where did you go? Who do you know?"

My heart started to spasm. I swear I could feel it.

Mr. Lawson cut in. "Which one?"

So I skipped right over it. "We moved here for my dad's work—"

Bobby totally interrupted. "What kind of work is that?"

"My dad's going to rebuild the original Houdini mansion, the huge one that burned down and then was totally taken over by hippies and ghosts." I started rambling. "Houdini never actually lived in the mansion, you know."

Bobby looked right at me. "You like magic?"

"I like invention." As soon as I said it, I could see most of them had no idea what I was talking about, but Trixie shook her head oh so slowly, like she knew exactly what I was talking about, like she thought about it all the time. And I wondered, Is she like me?

"And Mr. Houdini was one of the greatest inventors and marketers of all time," Mr. Lawson added. "All right, people." He clapped his hands, signaling school was back in session. "Find a buddy." He looked at me. "Charlie, we work the buddy system for the first few weeks of school."

I hated the buddy system more than life. You always got paired up with a total loser. "Love the buddy system."

Mr. Lawson pointed right at me. "How about you and Marta team up?"

See what I mean? My heart began to pound, my hands grew wet, I could feel all eyes on me, but most of all, I felt the old eyes of Scales. In my reformed heart, I knew that this was the moment—my fork in the road, people—offered up to me on a giant silver platter.

"Charlie?" Mr. Lawson called my name again.

I glanced over at Marta, totally about to say *yes*, when I was overcome with an involuntary hacking cough. Oh God, I couldn't do it. "I, I." Cough, cough—

Trixie raised her hand. Her nails were painted powder blue with specks of gold glitter. "Excuse me, Mr. Lawson," she asked like a meek little dove. Let me tell you, there was nothing meek or dovelike about her. "If it's okay with you, Charlie and I were already planning on being buddies."

Mr. Lawson nodded. He pointed to Babette. "Babette and Marta, team up, please."

Babs freaked; her face turned plum red, she kicked her desk and mumbled, "No, no, no, no."

"That wasn't a question," Mr. Lawson said. "Teams, go find a quiet place and start working on your first essay, 'What I Want out of Seventh Grade.'"

Trixie got her notebook. She was no girlie-girl. She wore camo pants and a pink tank top. I was totally digging her fashion sense. "Over there." She pointed, and I followed her to a small nook with pillows. We sat side by side, our new notebooks on our laps, both of us picking up our pencils, pretending to write.

"Thanks," I said, relieved.

"Yeah"—she glanced over at Marta—"she's harmless, but we stay away." She started writing in her notebook. *Okay, so who do you think is the cutest boy here?*

Bobby, I wrote back, then erased all trace.

She giggled. I wrote back. *What about you?*

"Sebastian," she whispered. "He's in tenth grade; he's Swedish."

"You'd make an awesome couple," I said, even though he could be a super ugly albino dog. It so wouldn't matter. Trixie would more than make up for it.

She turned the page as though she'd been writing and said, "Babs doesn't even like guys." She rolled her eyes. "She's so immature; it's like talking to a baby sometimes, you know?"

Easy, Charlie, easy. I could feel my heart race, but I knew better this time. "Yeah, but she looks really nice."

Her eyes got huge, her whisper deeper. "Have you lived in Europe or something?"

"No." I'm pretty sure she recognized my fashion greatness. But still, I had to ask.

"Why?"

"You look like a fashion designer." She checked out my seriously rockin' outfit. "There's something about you. You seem so"—she shook her head—"so unafraid, the way you put all that together. It's like you could care less what people think."

"Thanks." I think. I did a fashion sweep of the classroom,

and I was feeling all warm and fuzzy, and full of hope, until I locked eyes with Babette. Uh-oh. Man, did she look like she wanted to kill me. "She looks pretty mad." I nudged Trixie. "Does she hate me already?"

"She's lost without me." Trix waved to her like it was a job. "But come on, I can't do *everything* with her, right? It's a new year, and I want to meet new people like you. Is that so wrong?"

"No," I said, "course not." I tried to get down to writing, but Babette's daggers were shooting right at me. I waved and smiled.

When the bell rang for lunch at 12:30, I put my books away and was about to bite the bullet and find Marta when Trixie and Babs came running over to my desk. "Come on—I'll show you where we eat." Trix bounced up and down. "There's like twenty minutes, that's it, it's crazy how little time we get. In fact, when I run for class president, my whole platform is gonna be longer lunch."

"Yeah, longer lunch." Babette hung on her shoulder.

"Thanks, guys." I scanned for Marta's beehive. "And great idea on the lunch thing"—I had to come up with an excuse— "but you should go ahead. I gotta check on my little brother."

Total loser thing to say, I know, but far better than saying I had to find Marta.

Trixie gasped. "You have a little brother?"

"Yeah." I watched Marta kick her desk and growl at it.

"You are so lucky." Trixie was going on about the brother thing, "I wish I had a cute little brother. I'm the only one. Our house feels like a giant museum—"

Did she say "giant museum"? I was about to try to get an invite when I saw Marta's beehive at the door. "Gotta go," I said, and ran out into the hallway. I bumped and shoved my way through the pack of kids. And you know what? I loved it. No one knew me here. In Malibu you changed your tanning oil, your highlights, and they announced it on the loudspeaker.

"Marta!" I called her name, but she kept on going, that beehive just bobbin' along. Plus she had one of those Cinderella roller suitcases, so there was a massive space around her where people would not go. Or maybe it was because she smelled. I remained hopeful that she'd walk into the cafeteria and there, off in some dark corner, would be a table of horribly dressed, booger-eating, super smart outcasts just like her, even if they were second graders, it *did not* matter. I could tell Scales at our session next week that I'd found her, but she had a huge group of friends. And then I'd be done with Dr. Scales; no more talking about my feelings all the time, no more thinking about my words. Case closed.

But Marta did not go into the cafeteria. She went to the bathroom. I waited outside. It took forever. My stomach was growling, I was so hungry. I watched the kids going by; they were all so excited, the first day of a new year, all that possibility in front of them with no mistakes yet. Huddles of girls and boys comparing notes, computer games, talking about summer vacations and fashion icons. Oh man, I wanted in!

"Hey!" Trixie saw me hanging out by the bathroom and

came running up to me. "What are you doing there? Come eat with us." She pointed to the playground on the upper yard.

I pressed my back up against the door, like I was not stalking the person in it. "Who's 'us'?"

Trix played with her hair. "Well, um, the gymnastics team, some cool sixth graders, seventh too—" She stopped suddenly. "What are you doing?"

I swallowed. "Uh, waiting."

"There are other bathrooms here, you know?" She kinda of laughed, but I could tell she thought I was weird.

"Thanks." I faked a good laugh. "That girl Marta is taking forever."

"That's because she's not coming out." Trixie bounced up and down. "Come on, I want to introduce you."

"Wait a sec." I didn't move. "What do you mean?"

SPOILER ALERT: Trixie was way meaner than I ever was.

Trixie shrugged. "That's where she eats."

"In the bathroom?"

"Yeah." She started walking away. "And trust me, you don't want to use it when she's done. Her farts are legendary. They don't call her Marta the Farta for nothing."

And just like that I knew there would be no corner table in the cafeteria with booger-eating rejects like Marta. There was no doubt in my mind: Marta was always alone. I stood at the window and saw Trixie rejoining the kind of kids I wanted to hang out with but knew I'd never be able to once they saw me with Marta. Yep, I could feel it all slipping away.

"Hey, wait up," I called to Trix. It wasn't like Marta was coming out any time soon, so I might as well live in the moment. Carpe diem, right?

And so I spent the rest of the day pretending like this was a possibility for me. While Marta sulked around the place, Trixie and Babs took me around school, showed me the last remaining hiding spots, kissing spots, teacher-arguing spots, and even the place called Graffiti Alley behind the school where a hobo lived. By the time the bell rang, I had to say I could see myself becoming huge here. And we're not talking pounds, either.

After school, Pen and Felix were waiting for me at the front gate. I envied the heck out of them. If only my hands weren't handcuffed. If only I weren't wearing a straitjacket, courtesy of one very mean shrink, I could be happy, too.

Pen called out way too loudly, "Hey, Charlie, how was it?"

"Not now, Pen." I passed by them and started walking fast. Felix caught up to me and grabbed my hand when I wasn't looking.

"You were right." His freakishly bright blue eyes squinted against the sun. "My teacher is so nice, Charlie."

I squeezed his hand for a second and let go.

Dreaded Postmortem Family Dinner

Can I ask you something? Besides total butt-kissers like dear old Pen, what kid likes family dinner after their first (horrible) day of school?

My parents asked super annoying questions. Penelope, that eager-beaver pain in the you know what, jumped to go first, of course, because her day was always just so perfect. I could feel my hand gripping my fork all the tighter while she smiled and talked about how great her first day was and how many new friends she made because of the honor society she's been in since birth. Then there's the *Gate Group* for geniuses and the Honors Club for annoying do-gooders. And her millions of social causes, blah, blah, blah. If she sees a dead squirrel on the road, Pen starts a cause.

"And I'm thinking about spearheading an activist group

for inner-city literacy—" *Spearheading* was one of her favorite words. "And spearheading an outreach group to find gifted kids in impoverished neighborhoods."

The whole time I envisioned stabbing Pen in the forehead with my fork. All right, all right, don't call 911 or anything, I wasn't really going to do it. You can't say anything these days without being called into a shrink's office.

Felix already had two friends who invited him over both Saturday and Sunday. Whatever. He loved his teacher, yeah, yeah, yeah—

Dad looked at me. I was mashing my peas into a greenish paste. "And what about you, Charlie?"

"Oh." I smiled. "Great, it was just great."

"Did you meet anyone you liked?" he pried.

"I did." I told them about Trixie. How beautiful she was, how she had a huge house, which meant she probably had a huge closet, maybe even a wig collection. Have I mentioned how much I love wigs? She also had a pool, and she was an only child, *and* she loved my fashion sense.

"Anything more substantial than that?" Mom gave me that look, that look I hated.

"Mom, you'll be thrilled to know that my teacher wears those nasty Birkenstocks"—I glanced down at her feet—"just like you." But Mom wasn't biting. "And oh, I know, they celebrate diversity there." I took a long drink of water. "Now, may I please be excused? I have homework."

"Sit." Mom pointed to my seat. "Did you find her?"

"Um." I looked away. "You know, Mom, it's not that easy. It's not like people wear a shirt saying Biggest Loser, you know." I got up. "And you're stressing me out a lot. Can I please go to my room?" They were all looking at me like I was crazy. Who begs to go to her room? Someone who's been in solitary confinement, that's who.

"Just be nice to her." Pen shrugged. "It's not that hard. Like today I found this girl in the bathroom eating. Can you imagine that? She said people made fun of her food." Mom and Dad looked horrified. "So I took my food into the restroom and ate with her."

"What?" I stared.

"Yeah, Charlie, it's not hard," Felix said. "We're nice to you."

I threw my hand against my mouth and held my breath for fear that every swear word I'd longed to say would come pouring out in a never-ending stream and ran up the stairs and into my room. Why didn't they understand? What was wrong with them? With me? I collapsed onto my bed. "Oh, Mr. Mandela! No one understands me!"

Under my pillow was my laptop. I Skyped my friend Jai, who lived in an area called the Mumbai slums in the heart of Mumbai, India, lucky kid. He was so smart, he didn't even have to go to school anymore, which was totally unfair, because I was just as smart and I had *zero* free will. "Hey, Jai."

"Good morning, Charlie. How was your new school today?"

"Horrible."

He was sitting on the floor cross-legged, looking oh so fashionable in a white shirt. "Drop out like Gates, Charlie. Work with me. You're too gifted for school."

Right now I felt anything but gifted. "Yeah, yeah." In the background I could see his entire family, who did whatever he said because he was saving up to buy them a beautiful beach house on this tropical island called Goa where he said they could fish all day long and the rest of the time they'd prepare for tsunamis. God. Lucky him. Ever since he entered this competition set up by Interpol, the huge European version of the CIA, to find the best hackers out there, Jai had been fielding offers right and left. He was a rich and famous genius. His parents were his slaves, and he was twelve. Can you top that? I don't think so.

"Can I ask you something?"

His older sister served him tea. "Please."

"It's a conundrum."

"I'm good with those." He drained the cup and handed it back to his sister. She bowed and left. See what I mean? Pen would have thrown it at my face.

I explained my task, the task of Marta versus my own personal quest. "Okay, Jai, I'm gonna be straight. No matter how lame this might sound, I want to be popular—"

He shook his head. "A useless pursuit."

"But a lifelong dream," I admitted.

"Oh, Charlie." He bobbed his head; his little sister came in front of the camera and blew me a kiss. "You are too smart and far too funny. Why do you care for such silliness?"

"Jai, stop," I interrupted. "Just tell me, how do I do both?"

He was very quiet while he gathered his thoughts. Oh, this was going to be good! Jai could tackle any problem in a perfectly scientific way, so I knew he was going to give me something I could really, really use. Like an equation for popularity. And so I waited.

"Well, in my country, Charlie, good people like Mother Teresa and Gandhi were far more popular than those who just wanted the votes—"

"Whoa." I stopped him right there. "They died like a million years ago. How can they possibly matter to my own personal struggle?"

"Well." He pulled up a photo of each of them and split the screen. "In this country they are heroes."

Yikes, that's all I can say. They were some scary-looking people back then.

"They stood for something," he continued, "and it was this that made them hated at first, then loved later."

Whoa, whoa, hated? Who said anything about hated? "I can totally skip the hated part, 'cause guess what?" My nose tickled. "I'm pretty sure everyone hates me already, even here at home."

He shrugged. "Maybe it's because you're not nice to them, Charlie."

"I'm nice," I shot back.

He shrugged again. "Or you're terribly insecure."

I wanted to slap that Hindi accent right off his face. "Do I look insecure to you?"

For a while he said nothing. I was just staring at the screen. His whole family was moving around behind him while he sat with his legs crossed. After a while I thought he'd fallen asleep, and then his eyes jerked open, and he said, "You know something, Charlie? People, very important people, know about me through my work, but they don't know I am twelve years old. If they knew that, they'd never hire me, so when I converse with them, I simply pretend to be something I am not."

"You invent a new persona?"

"Yes, of course."

"But you don't lie?"

"No, because it is a new persona." He smiled. "You can be someone who cares about the bullied. You can make that your new persona."

Suddenly Pen came to mind. She had tons and tons of dumb causes. I bet when she came out of that bathroom with Marta, people thought she was a saint. "Like a cause."

"Mother Teresa."

I thought about it for a while. When you have a cause, people don't think you're doing it because you're a lonely loser; they think you're above it all, like you don't care what they think.

TRUE FACT: The key to popularity is not caring at all. Even Dr. Scales knows this one, and he's a dinosaur.

Like Pen. At our last school, she was so disgustingly popular, and she didn't care about it at all. "I'll go in there as the Mother Teresa of the bullied, obviously much better-looking and minus the massive wart. Thank you, Jai—you're a lifesaver!"

"Charlie, Charlie, hold on," Jai cautioned. "Whatever you do, don't go overboard. Go slowly, you must be balanced—"

At the sound of that horrible word *balanced*, I had to click off. I dived into Pen's closet, checked the hallway, then tiptoed to Mom's room to locate her jewelry box. Time to get my new outfit together. Think saris, think color, think jewels, think wow!

No One Did Anything, So I Did—My New Mantra

In an ideal world, I would have at least a weekend to switch personalities, because let me tell you, it is pretty tough going from someone who thinks about herself exclusively to someone who actually thinks about others. I had to access a side of my brain I've never really used before. By the time I finally made it down for breakfast, it was almost seven thirty.

Mom handed me a glass of juice and a piece of toast. "Baby, you have to go. The bell will ring in twenty minutes."

I turned. "Thanks." That's when she took a good look at me. "Uh, what is that thing on your head?"

"A *bindi*." I shrugged like it was simply the most obvious thing in the world.

Mom's face was a blank slate. She was struggling to understand. "What's a *bindi*?"

"It's like a third eye, Mom." I recited from the reading I'd done the night before: "It's about opening my consciousness up and creating a new pathway to compassion."

Dead silence.

I unfolded my scarf and threw it over my shoulders. Sadly I did not have the makings of a sari or even a tunic and Punjabi pants, but I did find leggings, a long white shirt, and a white scarf to wrap over my shoulders.

Dad watched me arrange my scarf. "Did you make that?"

"I did."

Dad drank the last of his coffee. "It's beautiful."

"Thanks, Dad." I got down on the floor, dumped out all my books from my faux snakeskin backpack, and put them in a white cotton bag Mom used for the shopping.

Pen was shaking her head. "Charlie, what's up now?"

I looked up at her. She had on a white man's shirt and a long skirt. Her hair was in a high, loose bun on top of her head, her pimples were uncovered, her brows unplucked. I could even see the shadow of armpit hair through her blouse, and you know what I said? "Man, you look beautiful, Pen." That's what I said.

Mom was quick to scold. "Charlie!"

But I was quick to correct, in a low, measured voice, of course. And PS, have you ever noticed how holy people are super slow (*but not boring*) talkers? Last night when I was watching Mother Teresa on YouTube, I was like, Wow, she almost seems stupid, *but* it's the opposite. The smarter you are, the more stuff's going on up there, the slower you are to speak. "No, Mom," I said slowly, "I think she looks beautiful." I stood. "Pen, last night I had an epiphany. *You* are my new role model."

Orange juice shot from Pen's nose. "Me?"

"Yes, you." I lifted her bag up and handed it to her. "Teach me to care about others like you do, Pen."

"But you hate charity! You take the money *out* of the UNI-CEF Halloween boxes." Pen laughed. Mom and Felix thought it was pretty funny too. In fact, all the laughter at my expense went on so long, I had to sit down. "Seriously, I don't know if it can be done, Charlie."

"Oh, come on, just teach me, for God's sakes," I implored. "You have so many causes, add me to your list, make me a cause." And then I got an idea. "I'll pay you."

"I don't want your money." Pen shook her head. "I don't even know what you want from me."

But I knew exactly what I wanted from her. "Like yesterday, when you went into that bathroom and ate with that weird girl, what happened when you came out, what did people say to you? How did they act? Did they run?" My fear. "Did they think you were a total freak?"

Pen shrugged like it was all so easy. "No, Charlie, they just thought I was nice, I guess." She was clueless about it, like someone who was naturally good. "I don't know. I honestly didn't even think about it."

"Wow." I needed facts. Hard-core facts. "Let me ask you

this. When you got out of there, do you think people liked you more or less?"

Pen closed her eyes, leaned back against the wall like she was dissecting her day, and then said, "More, people liked me more. I guess." She opened the door. "Can we go now?"

I jumped in front of her. "Last question, last question, I swear. Was it just the total freaks who liked you more or the cool people too?"

"Not that I see a divide, but I guess everyone. People felt sorry for her." She had this teary look in her eyes. "No one did anything," she said, "so I did."

"Wow," I repeated, "'No one did anything, *so I did.*'" Majorly catchy. That was it, my new mantra.

Meet Charlie C. Cooper, Selfless Activist

The bell rang just as we made it into the upper parking lot. Cars were pulling out. Horns were honking. Moms were yelling at moms; dads were running for cover; the principal had his loudspeaker—all with coffee mugs in hand, coffee teeth, angry lips. It was like my eyes had opened and I was seeing the world I lived in for the first time. I looked around and announced to Penelope, "So much anger."

Pen rolled her eyes. "I'm beginning to miss the old Charlie."

I pressed my little pink *bindi* jewel, making sure it stayed where it was supposed to, and then, as if it was a sign, Marta came walking up the hill wearing the socks and sandals again, her pants so short and tight, her massive calves nearly ripping them in two.

"Poor girl." Pen shook her head and walked into school.

I was just about to walk over to Marta when I heard Trixie shouting from the other direction.

"Charlie!" Trixie came running down the hill, Babs chasing after her. "I'm so late!"

"Hey!" I shouted back. "Hi, Babs." I waved to her too, because from now on I saw the Little Person.

Trixie's mouth dropped when she caught up with me. "Oh my God, I love your *bindi*!"

What! I stared. How great was this? "You know what a *bindi* is?"

"What's a *bindi*?" Babs pulled Trixie. "And by the way, we're late."

"I'm totally going Indian in every way," I announced, catching up with them.

"I love their fashion, their movies, their dances! Those women are so beautiful." Trix beamed.

"I know, right!" Babs concurred.

"Ever since I was a little kid, Mother Teresa was one of my heroes." I watched the look on their faces like, *What the heck is wrong with this girl?* But I persevered. "Being kind, doing stuff for the less fortunate, I just think it's cool."

Trixie shot me this look of horror. "But have you seen what she looked like?"

"Oh yeah, but I've totally updated. I'm going for the Bollywood thing plus the charity"—hand up to be clear—"minus the wart."

Kids streamed in and shouted across the now empty parking lot, "Hey, it's Marta the Farta!"

We all turned to see Marta, head down, pulling her Cinderella roller suitcase as fast as she could. It was like the gods were shining down on me. "See, that's what I'm talking about. Being mean to Marta; that's just gotta stop." I tried to sound like this was a sudden decision, not a horrifying task. "You know what?" I said as we ran up to class. "I'm going to stop it."

Babette shook her head. "Stop what?"

"Being mean to her," I said.

"But why? It's fun," Babs said. "Plus she doesn't mind at all. If she did, she'd dress better." Babs pulled open the door. "She'd cut her nails, look a little more human, *n'est-ce pas?*"

I let it go, because you know what? I was so not into having that kind of discussion.

TRUE FACT: Babs should have been on Scales's couch, not me.

Mr. Lawson strolled in with his chai tea in a brown, earthy mug. "Good morning. Call me Mr. L, and boy"—he zeroed in on me right away—"that *bindi* is beautiful."

"And super meaningful." I pushed on it hard with my finger.

"And it falls in so nicely with what we're doing this morning. All right, everybody." Mr. L smiled as if he actually liked us, which was pretty unusual for teachers these days. "Time to choose a community buddy."

"Community buddy?" Babs slapped the desk with her hands.

"Uh, you're kinda freaking us out, Mr. L." Trix rolled her eyes.

"Community building saves lives." He walked between our desks. "The buddy you choose will be your community-outreach partner."

Just the words *community outreach* used to make me feel like I'd been struck down with a deadly disease. But now, now, they validated my whole plan.

TRUE FACT: When you've finally hit upon the right course of action, the stars align.

I raised my hand. "Are we talking charity?"

"We are." He nodded. "But now we call it service. The word *charity* is no longer used."

"Kinda like *retard*?" Bobby yelled out. "Right. Mr. L?"

"Exactly, Mr. Brown."

He handed each one of us a list. "We're going to break into groups of two and choose the kind of service we want to do. All right?"

Babs jumped up. "I choose Trix," Babs announced before anyone else could say a thing. I looked over at Trix; she looked at me. She raised her hand, about to ask what I did not want her to ask.

I raised my hand higher. "Mr. Lawson, can I have"—I could barely get the words out, so I stabbed myself in the leg with the pencil and shouted—"Marta?"

Everyone laughed, like it was a joke. Trix looked at me. "Are you nuts?" Babs was smiling. Bobby kicked me under the table and said, "Good one."

"Nope, I choose her. I want Marta." I looked over at her, my new class pet. She was kinda snarling at me with her popcorn fangs. I should have brought bones.

It took a while, but Marta and I narrowed it down through an assortment of grunts that we were either going to work at the animal shelter or read to old people at the old people's home.

I dropped my head on the desk. "Come on, Marta, I can't take all those eyes staring at me from the cages."

"Old people's eyes are worse," she stated with a weird accent.

"Yeah, but they're supposed to die, time's up, clock's ticking. Those puppies are supposed to be adopted, Marta."

"Everything dies," she said with *zero* expression. Marta spoke each word like she wanted to slug you with it. Man, was this gonna be seriously unfun.

Trixie came around my desk, interrupting our heated debate. "Hey, guys, where are you gonna help out?"

"I want old people; Marta wants soon-to-be-gassed puppies."

"Babs and I are cooking at a boys-and-girls club," she said, laughing at us.

How come I didn't see that assignment? Babs showed up, leaned into Marta, like all of a sudden she liked her. "Hey, Marta."

But Marta just got up and slipped away, back to her desk. How could you blame her? If the mean girls at my old school were suddenly nice, I'd slip away too.

TRUE FACT: *Bindi*s don't have a lot of stick.

By the end of the day I had to use a glue stick to keep my poor *bindi* on. I saw Pen and Felix on the lower yard. Felix was playing a game of soccer; the older kids were trying to steal the ball, but Felix held on tight. This one kid who had to be twice his size even tried to kick him in the shin, but Felix, he kicked him right back. I was proud.

Pen was sitting with a bunch of girls. Some were playing with her hair; others were sitting by her feet, looking up at her and smiling or laughing at something she said. Marta was sitting on the ground over by the vegetable garden, writing furiously. Why was she trying to get her homework done so quickly? I wondered. What could a girl like that possibly have to do after school?

I decided to use this time to walk around and look for the biggest losers and try to make them feel like they weren't such losers because I, Charlie C. Cooper, was talking to them. Ugly girls and ugly guys were the ones I kept a keen eye out for, or the ones dressed in clothes that were so handed down, they looked like toddler outfits. "Cool Christmas vest," I'd say. "How was your day?"

"Go away, weirdo" was often the response. The word was out—I was friends with Marta the Farta. But you know what? I'm sure Mother Teresa had her fair share of tough cases too.

The yard had quieted down, and people were just waiting for their parents to come and get them. I was watching Marta, looking at all the knots in her hair, which she had clearly cut herself. She had these thick, uneven chunks of bangs. The back was hacked off like a wedge. Was it mange? Lice?

Trixie and Babs came down the stairs, slowing as they walked past Marta. Trix did a loud sniff like Marta smelled bad, which I had to admit she did.

Babs shook her head. "She smells."

Marta looked like a dog about to pounce. "*Grrrrr.*" She snarled her yellow-brown teeth at them.

"What's up, Marta?" Trixie teased.

"Yeah, what's up?" Babs followed suit.

Trix stood over her. "Toothbrush, Marta?"

"A little soap?" Babette shrugged.

"Deodorant maybe?" Trix stopped when she saw me coming.

I envisioned Mama T of Calcutta, took a huge gulp of air, walked over, and cut them off. "You know what, guys? Just leave Marta alone."

"What?" Trixie looked shocked. "We're just helping her out. See, the gymnastics tryouts are coming up, and poor Marta over here lost out last year because her personal hygiene wasn't what it was supposed to be, right, Marta?"

Marta looked right at Trix and growled.

"See?" Trixie shrugged. "I was just trying to help her along, that's all."

Marta stormed off without a word, and we all watched her leave.

Pen called me from across the yard. "Hey, Charlie, you ready to go home?"

Trixie and Babs turned and totally checked out Pen. She was so clearly in high school, it wasn't even funny. "Whoa, is that your sister?"

"Yep," I said. "Yo, Felix! We're going home."

"And that's your baby brother?" Babs put her hands to her face. "Ah, he's so cute!"

"See you tomorrow." I waved to them, and you know what? For the first time in a long, long time, I felt good going home with Pen and Felix. After I'd hung out with Marta, they seemed like rock stars.

We skipped all the way down the hill and waited at the crosswalk for the light to change. My nose started going crazy.

Something was in the air, a smell, a smell I knew and loved. "Mom made cookies!"

Pen rolled her eyes. "Oh, come on, how do you know?"

Felix shook his head. "Yeah, how do you know?"

"I'll bet you all your Halloween candy I'm right." I put my hand out. "And if I'm wrong, you get all mine."

"Don't do it," Pen warned.

The light was changing. "So you think I can smell cookies from this far?"

Pen shook her head in defeat. "You're so weird, it just might be possible."

The light changed, and I ran, my *bindi* flying off into oncoming traffic, my mom's shopping bag falling from my shoulder, but I made it to the front door just in time to see Mom leaning over the oven and pulling out a tray of cookies, a pitcher of cold milk and three glasses already on the table.

Mom's smile said it all. I was being rewarded for my new self, and you know what? Life was pretty dang sweet.

"Hey there, Mama T." Dad walked in, covered in dust, the blueprints for the house rolled up in his hand. "We broke ground." He came over and filled his palms with cookies.

Felix and Pen grabbed the rest. "Dad, you are such a pig! No way, you can't take all of them!"

"I'm in the trenches all day. I've been digging holes, looking for secret tunnels. I need cookies!" He reverted to his famous

Cookie Monster voice. Dad covered Mom in kisses, and Mom giggled like a girl.

She pushed Dad away. "Calm down—I'm putting in another tray." She opened the oven, and I was hit with that toe-curling aroma of baking cookie dough.

I went over to Dad and stole one of his cookies. "Hey, any luck on finding Houdini's tunnels?" See, according to the legend, Houdini hid all of his stuff in those tunnels, and people have been trying to get to them ever since—and not for all the right reasons, if you catch my meaning.

Dad drank my entire glass as payback. "Not yet, but at the rate the owner's got us drilling, we should hit them by the end of the week."

"Really?" I inhaled the kitchen like it was a fine perfume.

"Well, personally, I can't wait for the mansion to be built." Pen pulled out her books from her backpack and started organizing her work on the kitchen table, directly *in front* of us, all of which I found super annoying. "At least then I'll have my own room."

"Where's your sense of adventure? Your passion? Your own room, that's all you care about? Those tunnels hold the key to Houdini's magic." I took one of Pen's cookies, stared her down like a mean dog, and shoved the entire thing in my mouth.

Pen got this grossed-out look on her face and backed away. "Houdini's dead, and his magic is probably so old by now, no one cares." Pen shrugged like an old lady. "But my own room?"

She took a deep breath and looked up. "That's worth all of this."

Now that made me want to smack her. "You are so—"

Dad changed the subject. "Hey, how was school today?"

"I made two new friends," Felix announced. "Pete has a band in his garage, and Lucas can swear in Hebrew."

"Awesome!" Dad gave him a high five.

"And believe it or not, Charlie over here stuck up for that poor girl Marta when her new friends were picking on her," Pen took insanely tiny bites of her cookie. I wanted to smack her.

Everything stopped. Mom stopped baking; Dad stopped eating. "Wow," Dad said. "What a turnaround."

"I can't wait to tell Dr. Scales," Mom said matter-of-factly, and handed me a plate of my own.

"Yeah, yeah, yeah, blame it on the *bindi*." I ran up the stairs, cookies in hand.

I was not one for the spotlight, you know.

Assessing the Damages

So there I was, brand-new purple *bindi* in place, feeling like I'd made it.

TRUE FACT: I admit, my bindi is really just a plastic gem, left over from my bedazzler kit from fourth grade but blessed by yours truly.

All right. It's the end of week one, and it's time to take inventory, and if you don't know what that is, look out, man. It's called life.

So far:

1. I'd made zero enemies that I knew of.
2. Entered or tried to enter zero cliques.
3. Broke up zero friendships that I knew of.

Yep, so far I'd been nice to everyone, even Marta, who acted like an abused tiger ready to bite my sweet, caring hand. But she was coming around. I even let her pick the animal shelter where we're being forced to volunteer. But seriously, all this selflessness was wearing me out, dulling my senses, and all I wanted to do was spend my weekend doing stuff like digging holes and uncovering secret tunnels with Dad, or tracking down just how much cash President Putin of Russia had stashed away with my buddy Jai.

It was just after lunch when Mr. L sang out, "It's math time, people!" Which I thought was a pretty dumb idea. How can you force kids to concentrate two hours before the bell's gonna ring on a Friday? So there I was, sitting next to Bobby, checking him out as best I could without him seeing me, when all of a sudden I got the most horrible whiff of something so foul, my nose stung and my eyes watered up. I dropped the book. "What the—" I looked around. "What just died in here?"

Bobby pointed to his feet and licked his lips, like he thought he was hot or something. "Took my shoes off."

All I could do was shake my head at the stupidity of the opposite sex.

"My feet." He kept going on and on about it, like he was proud of his own stench, while Mr. L was going over fractions with a group of kids who actually wanted to understand them. What idiots. Like we're ever, ever going to need to know how to use a fraction. Fractions! Decimals! What century were we living in?

"These socks haven't been washed since school got out." He nodded proudly. "Last year, in June. I keep 'em in my soccer bag, wear them, put them back. My mom doesn't have a clue."

"Are you a complete psycho?"

"Charlie, Charlie, Charlie." He smirked. "I think you love me."

"I love *you*?" I screamed.

At which point the whole class turned to look at us. Gossip and laughter filled the room. Mr. L told everyone to calm down, then added like a jerk, "Valentine's Day is quite a ways away, kids." He smiled like it was funny. "Until then it's math and reading."

When the bell rang and everyone ran for freedom, Babette and Trixie came up to me. "Love him?" They grabbed my arm. "You love him?"

"Oh, please." I shook my head. "Bobby said it, not me, all right?"

"Oh, I know." Trix skipped along. "He's just trying to embarrass you."

"Whatever." I looked at them. I had so much bigger fish to fry, it wasn't even funny. I ran into the auditorium, thinking it would be a great place to hang out and devour the fantastic sandwich I had been waiting all day to eat. See, during lunch I had to sit with Marta in the bathroom, because she still wouldn't come out on account of the tuna fish sandwich her mom had packed her.

I don't know what was worse, the smells coming from the next stall or from Marta's nasty plastic-bag lunch. And it wasn't like she was thankful or anything. She basically totally ignored me.

I unzipped the zipper of my zebra-patterned insulated lunch box. Visions of the huge ham and turkey sandwich I'd asked my mom to make me tickled my tongue. My mouth was dripping.

But when I opened it up, all I saw was a cheese stick, a bag of carrots, celery, and some kind of horrifying brown-rice thing.

What the—*!!!* My mom was putting me on a diet without my consent.

Someone hit my shoulder. I turned and looked right into Marta's eyes. "What, Marta?"

"You can't eat here." She pointed to all the equipment. "It's starting."

"What's starting?" I got a good look at her outfit. "And what the heck are you wearing?" And then I knew. "Pajamas, really?"

She looked down at her fluffy bunny pants tucked into old cowboy boots. "Yeah, so what?"

The door opened. Why was the gymnastics team showing up?

"Stop stuffing your face, Cooper." One of the gymnasts pushed a gym mat past me.

Some dude slid past me with another mat. "Yeah, no food allowed."

I stared at Marta. My mouth dripped. I could smell the honey in the honey-baked ham. "But, but—" This was the cafeteria. Where else were we supposed to eat?

"Nope. It's the MPR, doofus, which stands for Multi-Purpose Room. It's the cafeteria, the auditorium, and the gym. All in one."

Boy, this was no Malibu Charter, that's for sure. There we had a dedicated cafeteria with a view of Zuma Beach and a self-serve fat-free yogurt bar.

Marta watched them leave with the look of death in her eyes. "Lillian's flunkies."

They moved so fast. Within minutes gym equipment came out from behind a curtain, mats were tossed on the floor, uneven bars were rolled out on wheels. Before our eyes, the boring old stinky cafeteria had been turned into an Olympic gym.

Marta watched. "This is one of the only schools with its very own competitive Junior Olympic team—"

"Wow, what a snob."

"No, you idiot," Marta snarled. "It means they're all levels seven and up and have a serious shot at qualifying for the Elites. Then it's on to the Nationals."

"Really?" Who would have thought that this little hippie

canyon school, where girls could be boys and boys could be girls, took gymnastics so seriously?

"And," Marta said, biting her lip, "with this coach, there's a chance, a tiny chance, someone might get chosen for a scholarship to go all the way." Marta said the word *scholarship* like I say the word Candyland, an all-you-can-eat gummy-bear candy shop near Universal City. FYI, it's where I want to be buried, which was happening sooner rather than later if I didn't eat my sandwich. They pulled down the banners, cleared chairs, and tossed all backpacks and lost sweaters into a room and closed the door. A balance beam was brought out, rings dropped from the rafters, even a trampoline appeared. A door opened, and wow! This girl/woman in the shiniest, most stunning silver leotard appeared; hair pulled back, silver head-band, silver earrings, silver slippers.

I couldn't take my eyes off her. "Who the heck is that?"

"Lillian. Team captain." Marta nodded, unimpressed. "Snap out of it, Coop. She's in our class; you see her every day."

But the transformation! I wanted to hate her—who wouldn't? She looked amazing, the attention to coordinating diamond and silver, the sparkly bits in her lip gloss, the all-matching silver accessories. We're talking five stars all the way. I watched her as she ran toward the mat and did flips in the air. "She's incredible."

Marta watched too, though she pretended not to. "Not as good as me."

I laughed; the more I got to know her, the more I knew that Marta could be pretty dang funny. She had this dry humor with a razor-sharp edge. We watched the rest of the team line up. They were impossibly long and lean; they didn't seem to walk on the ground. Lillian and her crew floated through the sky like shiny silver birds. But after ten minutes or so, Marta suddenly got up to leave. "The coach isn't even here. I need to see the coach." She stormed out with seriously unbirdlike steps.

I followed her, of course. "What do you want with the coach?"

"None of your beeswax," she said in a not-too-nice way, and left. I tried to catch Lillian and her gang of perfect people. Every school has them. At my last school they all looked like baby *Sports Illustrated* models: tanned, ocean-tossed blond locks, perfect bathing-suit bodies. Here, clearly they took the whole gymnastics thing way too seriously.

The door opened, and Trixie and Babs came in, hanging on to Lillian and company like those fish hanging off great white sharks. I leaned back in the darkened corner of the auditorium. There is nothing more satisfying than witnessing the girls you have to work so hard to get working so hard to get someone else.

And then something happened. Raised voices? A fight? I poked my head out for a better look and saw Trixie coming right at me. Her face was all red and her fists were tight little balls of anger. "Man, do I hate her," she hissed. "She's so full of it!"

"Who? What?"

Trix paced. "Lillian promised me." She was all steamed up. "No, she swore to me that she'd talk to Coach and get me a spot on the team this year for the uneven bars."

I immediately thought of Marta. "How many spots are there?"

"One or two, tops." She paced. "You have no idea how hard it is. Coach wants to take it to the Nationals this year to show the people who fired him what idiots they are."

TRUE FACT: Coaches with axes to grind are often fat, and red, and smell a lot like nail-polish remover. Just saying.

I was getting interested, 'cause, you see, I like a good back-story. "What's up with him?"

Trixie did a random handstand against the wall, just like that. "They totally kicked Coach off the Elite training team. They said he had no morals, whatever that's supposed to mean."

I bent over her. "You're turning a really ugly color, you know?"

"Blood to the brain is good." She flipped back down. "Anyway, now everyone wants on the team. He'll do whatever it takes to get us to the Nationals and then the Olympics." She clapped her hands together, looked up at the sky like an angel. "My face on cereal boxes! Me, Trixie Chalice, here I come."

Babs rubbed her shoulders. "Trix, you'll totally get the spot; you're awesome. You've been training all summer."

Trixie shook her head, full of doubt. "So have they."

Honestly, I found gymnastics to be so weird, especially the guys with those all-white bodysuits and bulging muscles. They were seriously uncomfortable to look at, if you know what I mean.

I looked at Babs, at Trixie, and said what Pen would say. "Well, all you can do is your best. You train, sleep, think positive thoughts—"

Trixie's little angel eyes suddenly got bigger and bluer. "There's also sabotage; they do it all the time in sports, you know."

"Yeah." Babs grinned from ear to ear. "Sabotage."

My ears perked right up at that word. I'd always loved that word, *sabotage*.

Trixie pointed at Babs and laughed. "Oh, my God, you should so totally see your face right now. I was kidding, Babs. Kidding."

Babs pretended to laugh. "You're funny, Trix."

Yeah, real funny. I wondered how far Babs would go to help her. I was beginning to feel more sorry for Babs than I did for Marta.

TRUE FACT: Followers are more dangerous than leaders. Just look at the dude who killed the Beatle.

Come Out, Come Out, Wherever You Are

Since I'd become the younger, prettier version of Mother Teresa of Calcutta, my parents were being so much nicer to me. It almost seemed a little fake, like they wanted to bask in the glow, if you get my gist, but we can't all be deep.

"You ready?" Dad asked me.

"Born ready." I got up, licked the maple syrup off my hands.

I couldn't wait—it was just the two of us. Mom had taken Pen and Felix to Malibu. It was just me and Dad.

I followed him over to his desk in the living room and put my chin on his shoulder while he studied the plans he'd made of the property, based on the original drawings of the mansion built in 1915. Watching them come to life reminded me that my dad was actually pretty cool, despite the Teva rock-climbing sandals he paired with socks and shorts when it got warm. Talk about a fashion faux pas that, I don't mind saying, strained the father-daughter bond in a dangerous way.

"We've already dug down eighteen feet over there by the house." He pointed to a spot right near all the bulldozers. "Nothing."

My eyes flew over the map. "What if the tunnels are so deep, you can't even hit them with a machine?"

Dad considered, glancing at the plans, nodding like crazy. "A deep hole and a ladder that takes you into a low tunnel. Genius. " Dad took a deep breath. "That could explain why we haven't hit it yet. We've been looking for a concrete structure coming all the way up to the surface."

I picked up the tool belt he'd made just for me, and we walked out into the sunshine and the quiet street traffic. "Imagine if we can find them in time for our massive Halloween party."

Dad gave me one of *those* looks. "What massive Halloween party?"

I grabbed his arm and screamed, "We live on the Houdini Estate, dude; of course we're going to have a massive party, and I want to invite the whole class, even the total dorks—"

Dad interrupted. "I was a total dork in middle school."

"Exactly. I want it to be like a giant welcome-to-the-neighborhood party."

My dad slipped his arm over my shoulders. "So living here is a lot better than Malibu, huh?"

TRUE FACT: In Malibu you were considered dirt poor unless your last name was Spielberg. If you didn't live in the Colony or at the very least on the water, popularity was a losing battle. If your dad redid old mansions wearing Tevas, it wasn't even a battle.

I turned to look at the land behind me, at the trees, the rock walls, palm trees, and the natural springs that bubbled up from underground somewhere. I thought about the tunnels and the ghosts and the magic that were just waiting for me. This was where I belonged. "I love it."

"And the whole Marta thing at school." He checked out the turquoise bead necklace I'd lifted from Mom's jewelry box and wore like a badge. "How are you doing with that?"

Over the mountain two red-tailed hawks began their dip-and-dive dance. I watched until they disappeared. "I'm not gonna lie," I said, "it's *hard*, so hard, like seriously HARD, but I'm giving it my best shot."

Dad touched my beads. "Just as long as you're not going to run off and join a cult."

"Cult." I looked at him, shocked. "A definite no, unless it is the cult of Coco Chanel or Vidal Sassoon. That man was a genius."

We walked up to a spot close to the top of the road near the gate. Dad pointed across the street. "There was a guest house there, with an elevator that went all the way down under the street and connected to the tunnels."

I scanned the area across the busy canyon road. I swear to God I could see it. The parties, the dresses, Houdini running as fast as he could from his ugly wife to all that fun. Man, imagine it, just imagine what could happen if I had an underground tunnel from my house to the school!

Dad dragged me down to the grass near the street. "And check this out. Way back when this house was built in 1915, the road was much, much smaller. The property came way out; they cut back the land on both sides to widen the street, which means the entrance could be closer to the street and not directly under the house."

He was right, the secret entrance could be in a totally different area than I'd been looking all this time. "Oh, man, two whole months down the tubes."

"But, but," he said, trying to cheer me up, "look what I got!" He pointed to a *monster* of an excavator. "Time to do some serious digging."

It was huge and ugly, its metal jaws ready to tear apart the earth. "With that thing?"

"Oh, yeah." Dad took off, and I followed. We got into the Caterpillar excavator and turned it on, and black smoke chugged from the exhaust. As Dad lowered its giant mouth, and it began to chew up everything in front of me, I got a seriously bad feeling, like *What the heck are you doing to my lawn?* Even if Houdini wasn't around anymore, were we being majorly disrespectful and would he be totally justified if he wanted to slash me in my sleep?

Dad yelled over the machine, "We're looking for concrete. If you hear it or see it, put your hand up, and I'll stop. Otherwise we could end up smashing the tunnel walls."

Smashing the tunnel walls? Built in the 1900s and hidden so beautifully for more than a hundred years? I couldn't do it, no matter how badly I wanted to find them. I put my hand up. He looked at me. "Let's stop."

"But, but you've been wanting to see them all summer." He gave me this weird look like he thought I was crazy. "I thought you'd love this."

Yeah, but this was seriously not cool. "On foot, with a flashlight, it's fair. But this bulldozing"—even the word made me cringe—"it just feels wrong, like I'm a big, mean, nasty hunter with a huge gun. It's just so, so *not* cool."

Dad said, "Okay," and turned off the giant machine. The smoke stopped polluting the sky, and I felt Houdini wasn't mad anymore.

Worse Than the
Spanish Inquisition

On Monday after school, I had Dr. Scales, *again*. I couldn't wait to tell him all about the road I'd taken on the path to self-realization with Mama T of Calcutta as my guide.

He kinda caught on when he saw my new outfit. I'd worked on it all Sunday. Mom took me to the farmers' market for fabric, ribbons, jewels, and bells, and you know what? I constructed a vision Karl Lagerfeld of Chanel would have stolen and copied: Picture Mama T, and if you can't, then Google her, you lazy people. I bejeweled a scarf like nobody's business. I can wear it over my head, around my waist, or even as a tube top. It's that great.

"Wow," he said, "did you create this?"

"I did. And all from the farmers' market, I might add."

"Ordinary people buy vegetables. You, Charlie, create a

statement. You've outdone yourself." He took off his glasses and looked me over. "Such an Indian flair to it as well. So exotic."

"And don't forget, holy as crap." I stuck a *bindi* on my forehead and on his—though on his it kinda got trapped in his giant folds of old skin. "I'm on a new path, Doc, one of peaceful kindness. I'm following in the footsteps of Gandhi, Mother Teresa, and my sister, Pen."

"I'm so glad to hear it." He sat back in his chair, pulled out my file, and opened it. "And were you able to locate and befriend *the one* everyone picks on?"

"Put it this way." I took a deep breath, trying to remain positive. "A blind man could have picked her out, it's that bad."

He nodded thoughtfully. "And have you managed to stay away from cliques, from your pattern of entering them by turning the members against one another?"

"Pattern?" I winced. "Come on, Doc, I wasn't that bad."

"Yes, you were."

"All right, fine." I removed my bedazzled scarf and laid it down on his desk. "The truth is that I have found that people actually like people who are nice." I fell back onto his sofa. "It's the weirdest thing in the whole world. You don't have to be cool, or even look cool. You just have to be seen being nice to total losers. Everyone just watches you and thinks you're like the nicest person, and they want to be around you. That's why Pen's so popular, you see?" I don't know why I never figured it out before, but it works. "It works like a charm."

He picked up his pipe, filled it with his tobacco that smelled both spicy and sweet, and put it in his mouth. "We all have our own roads, and we don't get there at the same time. You needed a fresh start and a pair of fresh eyes, Charlie."

"You're not gonna light that, are you?"

"No, Charlie." He puffed. "I quit, but I am still addicted to the process, the ritual. When we have bad habits, we often break them in stages, so don't be surprised if you find yourself repeating bad behavior subconsciously. It's part of the process."

"You know, there's a girl, her name's Trixie, and even though she has this weird thing for gymnastics, I think she and I could be major best friends."

"And does she already have a best friend?"

"Oh yeah, and it's downright sad." I got up and looked out the window. "If she got dumped by Trixie, I'm pretty sure she'd totally lose it—"

"Like you did?"

I was so not digging the comparison. "Yeah, whatever; all I'm saying is that I'm not doing it. No way. I see the opening to cut between them and I'm leaving it alone. I'm being nice to Marta the Farta, that's what I'm doing. And it ain't easy."

"I'm sure it's not."

I tapped my fingers on his desk. "So how much longer?"

He scanned my huge file. "Well, you've made remarkable progress, Charlie. You haven't pranked your sister since your last big one on June—"

Oh! I closed my eyes, cherishing every detail like the most perfect dream. I'd been kicked out for well over three weeks before school officially ended, and I was bored and yeah, okay, maybe a little bitter. Anyway, I felt like making a splash. I needed the diversion! *So* on the last day of school I executed a perfect prank. And even though it landed me in my room for a full twenty-four hours, meals placed outside the door, sister not talking to me, Mom glaring at me, it was so worth it—and not just for me but for the community. The response I got from all the poor, suffering middle kids out there, the ones just trying to catch a break, who were sandwiched between two painfully obnoxious siblings, was overwhelming. It carried me through those dark, post-expulsion days. And because I care about all *you* Suffering Middle Children out there, here it is: the Perfect Prank on Your Super Annoying Overachieving Older Sister.

1. Hack into your sister's school website. If you don't happen to be a natural-born computer hacker like yours truly, then wake up, people, and take a computer programming class. It's the future, and you don't want to be left behind.
2. Replace the school home page with one of the ugliest, most horrifying pictures you can find of your sister. For example, for my sister, Penelope, I used the one my mom took on the first day she got her braces. Her mouth was all swollen, bleeding, *and* she had a row

of fresh pimples along both sides of her nose. I'd been saving it like a diamond for just such an occasion.

3. Copy and paste headlines from your local humane society directly above the picture of your sibling. Good ones are: *No More Unwanted Babies Like This!* Or: *Neuter Her Now!* I put them right above Penelope's red, swollen brace face. And I tell you, it looked fantastic.

4. Count the seconds on your watch for the first bell to ring and the computers to be turned on. And bam, the entire school is looking at your little piece of art.

This was, as far as pranks go, well, let's just say I was proud. Think about it: Penelope's picture was on the screen of every computer monitor in the whole middle school. Every kid in that place, all fifteen hundred of them, flipped on their computers and got the shock of their lives: my sister, Penelope. Sadly, Penelope had just gotten her new cell phone. She called Mom almost instantly and, well, you know the rest of the story. Locked in my room forever. Mom and Dad took away all electronic equipment: computers, iPads, iPods, iPhones, even my brother's Nintendo DS, like I could hack into the school's mainframe with a Nintendo. Well, come to think of it, maybe I could.

"You look so happy right now, Charlie, almost angelic," the doc said. "What are you thinking about?"

I opened one eye. "Oh, just how much I want to help Marta."

He gave me this smirk thing like he wasn't totally buying it. "Well, if you can stay out of trouble and continue this new trend of taking the high road, then I'm hoping you'll be done with me before Christmas."

My stomach fell. "But Doc!"

"Charlie, you were in great danger if you kept up things the way they were. You have done a huge amount of work to see life through new eyes, but you must get to a stage where you simply own it."

"Oh, I do, I do own it," I protested. I just wanted to move on. *Move On!*

He glanced over at my beautiful scarf and beads. "Without the props."

"But I like props." Props make the world go around. Queens wear their crowns, armies their guns, what's wrong with my super sparkly scarf and beads from my mom's jewelry box?

"Yes, but they're props. You must own your new charitable self, like your sister owns hers. It's a part of her. When it's integrated in you, that's when you'll be ready to walk on your own two feet." He got up, picked up my scarf, and placed it around my neck. "I can't wait to see what happens with you. You've been given this second chance, Charlie, and you've taken it by the horns; you've been reborn." He shook his old fists like a boxer. "Take baby steps, not huge steps. You'll get there, I promise."

He walked me to the door, and as it opened I saw Mom

sitting in the same seat she'd been sitting in all summer long because of what I did. I stopped, looked up at his hairy nostrils, and remembered something I didn't want to remember. "The girl I like, Trixie, she knows people at Malibu Charter. You can't be reborn, Doc."

He agreed, but it didn't matter, 'cause all I could think about was what if Trixie wasn't so nice? What if one day she threw it in my face like a big whipped-cream pie?

It was something I had to think about.

Salad? Seriously? Can I Just Off Myself Now?

Salad, after a day in the trenches of middle school and on the couch with an old shrink getting your head shrunk, really, Mom? Is there no greater form of cruelty than salad? I bet even Mandela got more than salad.

TRUE FACT: Mandela got French fries.

"Carrots for your eyes, beets for your brain, and lettuce for your intestines, Charlie." Mom prepared the platter of death. "Live food, raw and all from my garden."

Puke, puke, and more puke.

"That's right, roughage," Dad chimed in like he was part of a tag team. "When your mom and I were young, we back-packed all over Thailand and even became vegan."

We all rolled our eyes, of course. What kid likes the *Before You Were Born* stories? Grown-ups do this to prove that they were once cool. But they weren't, not even then. Case in point: Who backpacks anywhere when you can drive?

"Well, I love steak," Felix said.

"Oh, Dad," I said, jumping in. "Have you thought more about the Halloween party?"

Mom put down the huge plate of vegetables, which of course no one touched but her. "I think it's a great idea." Mom's teeth were now studded with carrots. "Your dad and I have been working on it all week—"

Dad cut in with a creepy smile. "We're digging graves." Then he added sound effects. "Ho, ha-ha-ha."

Felix went white. "Graves?"

"And filling them with dead people." Mom put down another plate of something green; and green, unless it's a gummy bear, is never good.

I poked it. "Mom, what is *that*?"

"Zucchini frittata," she announced with pride, "made from the beautiful zucchini we bought together at the farmers' market. I added eggs and a little Parmesan cheese."

The thought of it made me want to cry; all that cheese wasted. Plus it was time to check the latest updates on cyberbullying and teen blackmail. I was on the other side of it now, working to end it. Also, I wanted to give Jai an update. "May I be excused?" Pen's mouth was full of that nasty frittata; so were

Mom's and Dad's. "I have stuff to do."

I got the okay, dumped the dishes, and ran up the stairs. Within seconds I was stretched out on my bed, laptop on my lap, feet up, hand in a secret stash of candy, in absolute quiet. Now this was happiness. I did a quick check of the latest news in cyberbullying—nothing new there.

TRUE FACT: Uh, people, if you don't put yourself out there on the net, you can't get cyberbullied.

Jai's world, on the other hand, was fascinating. When I Skyped him, he was wet with perspiration like he'd just come off a coding session that worked him like the superstar he was.

"Busy day?"

"It's these bloody markers. Their system's been compromised; the government's freaking out." He scooped up some lentils and rice with a piece of bread. "And we've had the monsoons here. It's been hot and wet; mosquitoes are carrying malaria all over the camps."

I felt lucky and sad. "Is there anything I can do?"

TRUE FACT: Markers are like bugs that enemies use to infect your computer systems. It's how they (we) spy on foreign governments and how they spy on us.

He suddenly got closer to the screen. "Wait, is that a *bindi* on your forehead?"

"Don't laugh." I got in full lotus position and broke it all down for my Indian brother. "Wearing the scarf of kindness, the beads of calm, and the good old third eye of wisdom has made me impenetrable. They don't even ask me why I'm nice to all the poor friendless saps out there. They just think I'm weirdly nice to them and don't question my motives. It's really beautiful."

Jai paused and then said, "When I see someone who is kind to someone he does not need to be kind to, I don't question it either. I question myself for not being kind"—he nodded—"so I suppose your random act of kindness highlights their lack of it. It embarrasses them, so they say nothing. Very clever, Charlie, very, very clever."

"You helped big-time, Jai." I yawned, curled into my bed, and couldn't wait to sleep. "I really owe you—"

"Yeah, yeah, yeah," he said. "Over and out, Ms. Cooper."

I could barely keep my eyes open, so I just mumbled, "No one says that anymore."

Jai winked and was gone.

Mr. L's Freakishly Hairy Nostrils

As soon as the bell rang, Mr. Lawson stood in front of us and let just one word fall from his mouth. "Competition." And then he walked back to his desk and sat down. We all stared at him, looked at one another, all wondering if Mr. L had dementia *or* if all that nostril hair was actually clogging his brain somehow. Not that I'm a doctor or anything.

"Uh, Mr. L." I raised my hand. "What do you want us to do?"

"I want you to think about the word. Quietly. Thoughtfully. What does it mean to you? What does it mean for us as a whole?"

Erica in the back groaned. "Can't we just take a multiple-choice test, a sample CST or something?"

He took a deep breath and held on to the desk. "This school

follows the constructivist method, pioneered by the great John Dewey. We build thinkers, not memorizers. Charlie"—he pointed—"you first."

"Well, to be perfectly honest, I hate competition," I said. "I think it turns us into cannibals, which isn't so hot for the community as a whole, if you know what I mean."

"Wow," he said, clearly impressed. "Very strong."

Marta turned and glared. "Competition is the very backbone of the human race. It's a race, people, and the best must win."

I glanced over at Marta. Pretty heavy stuff.

Lillian played with a pencil. "Imagine if we all competed in looks, and only the best-looking survived. All ugly people would be gone, poof!" She smiled at Marta. "So much better, right?"

All the guys clapped. Then all the girls clapped, except for the ones who knew they were ugly. And me, I did not clap.

"Oh, stop!" Babs pretended to quiet everyone down. "Charlie's not laughing. Charlie and Marta are definitely *not* laughing."

I wanted to punch her in the face.

"All right, all right, we're getting off track. The reason I'm asking you this is because we have gymnastics tryouts coming up." The room exploded. "And as you all know, at Happy Canyon there is nothing more heated than the tryouts. But this year, Coach is looking for that diamond in the rough, the one who will go all the way." He surveyed the room. "So this is about competition with others but also competition against yourselves." Lillian raised her hand. "Yes, Lillian?"

"We"—she stood, her eyes roving, her voice rising in excitement—"finally have a chance to make it all the way to the Nationals." The room exploded into foot stomping and screaming. "With our new coach, there's no way we can fail."

"Don't forget"—Trixie shook her finger—"you still need someone who can pull off the uneven bars."

Lillian looked right at Trixie. "You know what competition is, Mr. Lawson? You do it with all you've got; you try every last thing to get what you want, because you want it more than you want anything else in the world."

Marta nodded, like some kind of Jedi knight or freaky serial killer. I saw something there and then, a powerful secret brewing like trouble in those sleep-encrusted eyes of hers. I wanted in.

She Loves Me!
She Loves Me Not?

Later that afternoon I slipped into gym practice to see what everyone was getting all worked up over. Except for the spotlights on the mats, the room was dark and cold. There was no noise except for the slap of a mat, the hard, fast running of a vaulter, and the yelling of the coach. From a darkened corner, I watched them like a fly on the wall. Erica was tall and about as limber as a rubber band. She was so beautiful to watch; you almost forgot she probably ate babies for breakfast. Her cartwheels were like the slow spin of a wheel. Precise and exact. The girl called Tanya was fast and short, all power. Lillian was a perfectionist. But Monique was the worst of the bunch. Even I could tell she was sloppy. She put on lip gloss and checked her phone more often than I breathed. I bet she would be the one they'd drop first.

Lillian was mad again. She screamed at the team like an evil stepmother. "You're so fat; you look like a slob!" She berated Monique on her floor exercise. "Coach will throw you off if you keep it up."

When I turned to leave, I almost missed Marta sitting behind the curtain. In her eyes was an intensity that was almost scarier than her pink socks and Crocs. Was she just obsessed with being like Lillian, was that it? I could totally get that; Lillian was everything she wasn't. But in Marta's eyes there was more than envy. I couldn't figure it out. Did she really think she could do this? Marta? She was such a klutz, she could barely get down the stairs without tripping over her roller suitcase or the backs of someone's shoes.

Oh, poor Marta, I thought as I saw the pained look in her eyes. How long have you been hiding in here and fantasizing about being Lillian? It made sense; I would have hidden in here too if I were Marta. I was just about to go over to her when the door opened and a triangle of afternoon light came in. Trixie called me over. "Hey, Charlie, want to come to my house?"

My heart leaped—her house? "Your house?"

"Yeah"—she pointed—"it's just up the road. You can walk home after if you want to, or my housekeeper can drive you home. Here"—she handed me her iPhone—"call and ask."

My God, I loved her. What a self-starter, what an independent, what a cool chick. I called, and when my dad answered, I turned my back to Trixie. There was no dignity in begging.

"Hey, Dad. Can I please, please go over to Trixie's today? She invited me."

"Is her mother there?" Dad asked right off the bat.

"Her housekeeper, who is basically like her mother, is there, we can walk, it's super close, and"—I walked away so Trixie wouldn't hear me—"I will so cut both my wrists if you don't let me go. Please, Dad, please."

"Well, your mom isn't—"

"Dad, please. I've done everything you wanted me to. Please, please."

There was total silence on the line. And then he let out a deep breath. "All right, just call me when you get there," he said matter-of-factly. "And have fun."

I can't tell you how those words warmed me. "Thanks, Dad."

Trixie's Mega-Mansion, Here I Come

I handed her back the phone, and we started walking up the hill. "So, you like gymnastics, huh?" she asked.

I was huffing and puffing like a fat, old man.

Trixie increased her pace. "It's life or death to some people here. You just wouldn't believe what they'd do to get on that team." She turned, and we started walking up narrow Wonderland Park Avenue to Trixie's house, our book bags low and heavy. "The new coach was really famous once. His name is Igor Nemov; he coached the top teams in Russia, came here, and was on the Olympics path."

All this Olympics talk made me want to get to the nearest sofa and crack open a *giant* bag of Doritos.

"Coach got into a huge fight with Big Bela, who controls the Olympic team; they fired him, and Pickler hired him to start a team here. It's the first of its kind."

Boy, I so did *not* care. But I pretended to care.

HELPFUL HINT: People, you must pretend to be interested in whatever your new friends like, even if you couldn't care one bit.

So I glanced over, wiping the puddle of sweat off my forehead, and I asked like I really cared, "The first of what kind?"

"A school with its very own Junior Olympics team. He's grooming it to be the best in the world."

I shrugged. "I thought it was just a school."

"Are you kidding me?" Trixie laughed. "Every gymnast in LA wants to come here for the opportunity to train with the great Igor Nemov."

We walked more. I had to stop and catch my breath. These hills were killer. "Yeah, even Marta. She was watching the team and looked a little scary."

"Yeah, poor Marta." Trixie rolled her eyes. "She's delusional; she actually thinks one day she'll make the national team and go all the way. Last year she made such a fool of herself. She wore this horrible leotard—it was all stretched out and faded, and her hair was a wreck. She got tossed out before she even tried out, because you have to look good, right?"

"Of course!"

"Anyway, her face turned bright red. She totally flipped

102

out; she screamed in a weird language; it wasn't pretty."

And then it came to me. Maybe Marta was a complete nut. Maybe I could be relieved of my duty altogether! And by the way, man, was it fun to gossip. "Can she even do gymnastics?"

Trix laughed. "Poor thing can't even walk the stairs without tripping."

Wasn't that the truth? I definitely needed to hook her up with Scales. We kept walking up, up, up, like two sweaty teenagers, and I was feeling like I was about to seriously explode from the swelling I was experiencing in my fingers and toes, when she said in a totally cool movie star voice, "So how long were you at Malibu Charter? You did say Malibu Charter, right?"

My hair went up like a cat's, yeah, that's right. Had she been Googling me? I changed the subject. "I'm dying. How much farther?"

She pointed to the tight left turn. "Oh, come on, tell me. I can find out in a second, you know."

She was right, of course, there was no use in hiding it, but the trick I was trying to pull off was to get her to not even *care*. "Yeah, Malibu Charter." I pointed to a house with a drawbridge. "What's up with that?"

Trix's eyes popped. She smiled, like she'd just gotten ahold of something really good. "So you were there when that girl put laxatives in the lunch food, and the school exploded in diarrhea?"

Now it was getting a little sticky. I couldn't lie, 'cause everyone in the entire city knew about it; forget the fact that I was the one who did it. "Yep, I was."

Trixie grabbed my hands, thrilled. "Oh my God! You know, I go to summer camp with the girl from Malibu Charter who was the best friend of diarrhea girl before she went psycho and poisoned the whole school." She laughed like it was funny, which it wasn't.

TRUE FACT: Roxy should have been the target of my wrath, not Ashley. She was not a true friend. I know that now.

I laughed, pretending to act surprised and interested in all her little details of my downfall, but all I could think about was how long I had until she called Roxy and told her she knew me. Trixie would then have all the ammo she'd need to make my life miserable when the time came. Sadly, the time always came.

We walked up a steep bend and then veered off to the right. A car came speeding past. "Watch it!" Trix threw her hand in front of me and pushed me off the street. "They're maniacs around here."

The thought of getting hit by a car came as a welcome relief.

"Roxy told me they actually tried to put that girl"—Trix stopped—"what was her name?"

"No idea," I said.

She kept walking. "I'll find out. Anyway, they wanted to put her in some kind of mental facility, but they couldn't, so they kicked her whole family out of the school district. Can you imagine getting kicked out because you have a crazy sister?"

I thought of Penelope and how much she hated me for it. "No, I can't."

Trixie cocked her head and gave me one of those sideways looks. "You know what I think?"

Uh-oh. Here it comes.

"She's kind of a coward."

"Coward?" I jumped at the word. I was many things but not, I repeat, not a coward.

"My sources said she would have totally gotten away with it if she hadn't tried to stop the kindergartners from eating it. Seriously?" Trixie looked at me like she knew it was me. "I mean, really! Follow through; if you're gonna do something, at least follow through!" She pointed to a huge, towering block of white capitalism and announced, "This is me."

I melted. "You?" I stared at it like it was a castle in the desert. "Lucky you."

SPOILER ALERT: Her name wasn't Trixie for nothing—that girl was born with tricks up her sleeve. But then again, so was I.

Her housekeeper answered the door, and—wait for it—we rode up in an elevator, yep, you read it right, Chica, *elevator*. It opened onto a room of cream carpets, cream sofas, and curtains. I was practically speechless. There were huge paintings with splotches of bright color and a single family photo of three, just *three*.

"My parents are both shrinks." She pointed to a series of super serious double doors. "They work in there." She paused heavily. "They *live* to help people."

The house was so dang silent. "Are they there now?"

"Yep. But they have a separate entrance." Trixie shrugged. "And it's soundproof. See?" She screamed at the top of her lungs and no one noticed at all. Not even the housekeeper came to check on us.

It was grand! No one cared—imagine that?

She took my hand, and we ran to her palatial room. My mouth fell open. My God, was life unfair. Her closet, her clothes, her *king-size* bed! I mean, kill me now. A pop star could live here. She threw her stuff on the floor. "Just drop your things here," she told me, and I did. Within minutes the uniformed housekeeper came in with a tray of cookies and milk just for us. It was so quiet in here; the truly peaceful life of an only child. If I lived in this perfect room, I could be the next president of the United States or Russia if I so desired. Or a top model.

Trix plopped onto the bed. "So tell me, what are your talents, Charlie Cooper?"

"Besides compassion and fashion?" My new motto.

Trixie pushed on the *bindi*. "Yep."

"I know my way around a computer."

Her eyes lit up; she picked up her laptop. "Oh, oh, add me as a friend!"

Now here's where I thank God in heaven my mother never allowed me to get a Facebook page. There would be no escaping my past. "I don't do Facebook—"

"What?" She looked totally freaked, logged on, and up popped her page. I quickly looked at her pictures, and my heart fell through the floor when I saw none other than Roxy Daly's face. I hadn't seen her since the day I'd been expelled from that school to a standing ovation. Her last words, *You can run, but you cannot hide, Cooper.*

Trix saw my face. "Oh yeah, that's my friend Roxy." She went to Roxy's page. "She's the one who I told you about who went to your old school." Then her face got all crinkled up. "It's kinda weird that you don't know her."

"Yeah, well"—my face was getting hotter by the second—"I was in a special section, gifted—"

Trix gave me the look. "Oh, please, don't tell me you're gifted."

I knew that look. It was the way I looked at my sister every day. "No, God no, the total opposite. They just put me in there because of the computer stuff."

Trixie clicked off and rolled onto her back. "Well, she's a

super cool girl, Rox."

The thought of her still made my heart hurt. I loved her, I did. I'd never forget that first day of kindergarten when we were five years old. I walked into the room, wearing the outfit I'd been planning all summer, and I saw her, and she saw me. Something passed between us, like we both knew at the exact same time that we were going to be best friends, with the whole world waiting just for us to team up and take it over.

Cut to six years later. The friends you'd known all your life, the ones you locked eyes on all those years ago, split BFF necklaces with, had sleepovers at each other's houses, *could not live without*, they ran away from you, lied about their birthday parties, crank called you from those very same birthday parties no one told you about. Horrible.

Trix shook me. "Uh, hello. Earth to Charlie, come in, Charlie?"

I took a deep breath, looked around the room, and remembered that was then and this was now. It was all over and would *never* be repeated again. *Ever.*

She jumped up on the bed. "So team tryouts are coming up. There's gymnastics, of course, and soccer; there's even basketball." She looked me over in a not-so-flattering way. "You'd be really good at basketball—"

"I'm not into competition." Truth was I never tried out for a team in my life. At my last school, everyone did surfing, which was one of the stupidest sports in the world besides golf.

Freezing water, hungry sharks, and huge waves that dragged you along the rocky ocean floor. How stupid do you have to be?

She stretched her legs over her head. "This year I'm making the team or I'll kill someone, swear it." She bounced. "There's one spot open, and it's mine. Lillian promised me, so I have nothing to worry about, right?"

"Yeah, right," I said, but in all truth, she was looking a little creepy.

Trixie got up, pulled open the double doors to her closet, found an entire basket of bathing suits, and tossed them on the bed. "You feel like swimming? The pool's on the roof."

Pool—did someone say *pool*?

When I got home, I was faced with a huge hole that took up the entire yard. Dad was hunched over his plans, all sweaty in his shorts and jean shirt. Not exactly Trixie's house, that's for sure. When he saw me coming down the driveway, he put aside his shovel and gave me this funny look.

I laughed. "What?"

"You know you're acting like you're sixteen these days, with all this independence, walking to and from school and your friends' houses." He gave me a huge hug. "Your hair's all wet, you smell like suntan oil, you're smiling—where's my kid Charlie?"

"What can I say?" I gave him a kiss and opened the door. I was hit by a wall of odor so delectable, so wonderful, it made me stop cold. I sniffed the warm air like a hound. "Oh Mom, oh Mom. What is this ambrosia?"

"Polenta with Gorgonzola. Happy?"

"Ah, thank God." Now we were talking.

Mom came over and hugged me. "How was Trixie's house?"

How to put this without going over the top? *Vogue* magazine worthy. Creamy perfection, only-child attention to neatness, a housekeeper called Esmerelda who served us snacks while we floated on silver and gold rafts in the rooftop pool—"

Pen walked into the kitchen in her pajamas, opened the fridge, poured some juice. "Elitist pigs."

Mom interrupted. "Penelope—"

"A kid being served while floating in a pool is savage," Pen said, outraged. "We're raising a bunch of entitled kids who use the Mexicans as labor and then want to kick them out. This country has lost its way."

I just stared at her. Seriously. Can I please catch a break over here; must she always fight for the little guy? What about me?

TRUE FACT: I did not see Esmerelda spit in any of the food whatsoever, which is what I would have done if I didn't like the bratty kid of my employer.

Pen's face got all scrunched up. "And on top of it all, I think Trixie Chalice is using you."

"Using me?" I laughed. "Did you not hear she has a pool on

her roof? A dedicated servant by the name of Esmerelda? What could I possibly have that she doesn't?"

"I've been watching her." Pen inhaled like she meant business. "She's mean, on the lower yard when you're not around; she's a bully, especially to Marta—" Pen paused.

"Not everyone can be held to your standards of Amnesty International, Pen." I grabbed a glass of grapefruit juice, my absolute favorite. I downed the glass.

"Marta is the punching bag of the entire school because she's from a poor family; she's not from here—"

Pen was getting all red and foamy like she was gonna stroke out.

"I got it," I said just to shut her up. Sure, it was all true, and I did feel sorry for Marta. Heck, I practically adopted her and her toilet every day at lunch, but wasn't I allowed to have a little reprieve, a little rooftop fun? *Ever?*

I went to the fridge. Inside were little batches of cut carrots and celery. "Oh, come on, carrot sticks?!" I grabbed the tray and shoved as many carrots as I could in my mouth.

"She doesn't wear underwear, Pen—"

Pen winced. "Never?"

"She says she doesn't agree with them." I watched Mom laugh. "So," I continued, "if you don't wear underwear and haven't brushed your teeth since the other ones fell out, chances are you're gonna get teased."

"Look, I'm not saying she's not a perfect target," Pen said, mellowing out. "I'm just saying I'm thinking about spearheading a group at school to stop after-school bullying."

How was it possible we came from the same parents? "You do that, Pen." I got up to go, and then I remembered something. "Oh, and check this out. Trixie knows Roxy." I watched the name fall like a grenade on the kitchen floor.

Mom turned slowly from the stove, even dropping the spoon into the polenta, a major polenta crime. Pen's face looked like an ugly possum caught in front of a truck. Dad and Felix pulled open the door and walked in, covered in dust from the digging, and took in the scene. Total silence.

"What's going on?" Dad asked.

Pen, of course, couldn't wait to be the first to tell my story. "Trixie knows Roxy."

Mom shook her head. "How does she know her?"

"UCLA surf camp," I said, feeling a little tight. "They do it together every summer."

"It's a small world." Dad shook his head. "I always tell you kids that."

"Get another spoon or take the polenta off the burner." I watched the spoon drown and disappear in the bubbly goo. "And no, people, she doesn't know it was me. Not yet anyway."

Mom grabbed a wooden spoon and fished the old one out. "She'll call her and ask."

"If she hasn't already," Pen said.

"If she knows already," I countered Ms. Smarty Pants, "why

didn't she say something?"

Dad filled his glass with a sun tea Mom made that smelled like old socks, but not as bad as Bobby's socks. "Either she hasn't called her yet, or she knows and is fishing to see just how badly you want to keep your past your past. If I were you, I wouldn't get on her bad side."

"I don't plan on it," I said, and meant it.

"Or come clean." Mom dished out the warm polenta into deep bowls and crumbled a little Gorgonzola on the side. "Tell everyone what happened."

"Don't you dare!" Pen took her bowl and sat down.

Dad shook his head. "Bad idea, babe."

"Yeah, over my dead body." I glared at them over my bowl with extra cheese.

Then Pen started to get really worked up. "What if she's holding out? She knows it was you and is keeping that information in her little pocket to take out when she needs to bribe you."

"Or burn you," Dad added, just for a sunnier picture.

"But she isn't like that." Oh, the sweet corn taste, the pudding like quality, the cheese. I was almost done. "She's not perfect, okay, but she's actually pretty funny and nice."

"Lord oh lord, Charlie, for a person so smart, you can be so stupid," Pen said, and walked off.

The rest of them were just kind of sitting there, heads lowered like they knew something bad was coming and I was too blind to see it. "Well, even if she is using me, I've got nothing that anyone like her could possibly want, so it's fine by me. In the meantime, did I mention she has a pool on her roof? And a full-time, dedicated housekeeper just for her?" They were silent. "Now I've got some programming to do." I took a hand-ful of carrots and went upstairs to check on my good friend Jai.

Competition Gets Ugly

The first week of October marked the beginning of team try-outs, and let me tell you, the place was a nuthouse. Everyone was on edge. It was seriously cutting into my spiritual journey. But the good news was I'd come to the conclusion that Marta was delusional. Like seriously delusional. Let me explain.

So there we were at the horrible no-kill animal shelter down in Culver City, where the dogs were divided into puppies, bullies, and the ugly ones no one wanted—sounds like Malibu Charter, right? Anyway, Marta and I were cleaning out the gobs and gobs of poo from their nasty pens when I decided to bring up the whole gymnastics thing. Now, I'm no shrink or anything, but she had me seriously worried.

First of all, she truly believed she was going to the Olympics. She could barely sweep and walk at the same time, and she was telling me she was Olympic material. She was going on and on about all these complicated routines she could supposedly do, and I was like, *Please, how stupid do I look?* Mind you, she didn't talk to me like she liked me; she just barked at me like a mad dog.

Scales had told me that was to be expected from someone who's been bullied, and, more importantly, he'd said even if it's a total one-way street of her yelling at me, it still counts. So I just listened to her go on and on like a crazy homeless lady, telling me about her gymnastics fantasies while we mopped up poo. How this qualifies as "community building" I'll never know.

TRUE FACT: All they do is use us schoolkids. Community service is slave labor, that's all.

"I'm trying out this year, and no one is stopping me." She wiped her nose on that pink velour sleeve of hers. "Last time the cowards, the fakes, they kept me from showing them what I can do, what I was born to do." She was getting really into it; her face was all red and sweaty. "All they can do is make fun of the way I look. Well, I don't care about the way I look."

You know what I was thinking? Maybe you should. Care, that is. What's wrong with caring about the way you look? Fashion and compassion, remember? But then I had a thought. Maybe Marta looked like this because she came from

116

a fashion-impoverished culture. "Marta, you're not from here, right?"

Her face got all scrunched up. "Why, what do you care? You gonna do something, huh? You wanna run to Trixie? You people have no idea who you're messing with." She was really getting revved up now. "Just wait until it's my turn. Nothing, I repeat, nothing will stop me from going all the way. They will all come begging for me."

See what I mean? She seriously believed in her head that she could do gymnastics. It was like me thinking I could be a tightrope walker. I should have called the loony bin ASAP, right? But as "compassion" was my new middle name, and I was weeks away from saying good-bye to Scales for life, I didn't want to rock the boat. Plus I had to admit even I couldn't wait to see her in action.

When I saw Scales, I recounted the entire episode word for word in the hope that he would see that she was insane and set me free. But you know what he said? "You could be right, Charlie." He thought out loud. "Or she could be an amazing gymnast—who knows?"

I shook my head. "No, Doc, she's nuts, and because she's nuts I'm pretty sure I should be let off the hook." Then I threw in, "She could even be dangerous."

He shook his head. "It feels to me like she could be even more complex and worthy of your help. Perhaps it is true"—his eyebrows were getting all twisted—"perhaps she was barred from tryouts last year because she didn't look as good as they did."

I jumped up. "Well, fashion matters, Doc. Have you ever seen a sloppy gymnast?"

"Then help her." He leaned back. "If she's talented, it will change her life."

Why was it every time I came here with a solution, the man gave me another problem? "Now what do you want me to do?"

He sharpened a pencil and watched the shavings curl like it was an incredible event. "You said it yourself once: Fashion is your life. Help her."

"I can't help her." I jumped up and stomped. "You should see her!"

But he did not care a bit. "Until next week."

"I hate you," I mumbled.

"I know." He opened the door, and my dad took me home.

The Day Marta Would Never Live Down

Today was the day. Team tryouts after school. Sweat rings, shiny outfits that rode up your butt, and hairy pits. Need I say more? But I had come to support Trixie and pick up the pieces of Marta, which would be my final act of kindness. I was going to be their personal cheerleader waiting in the wings, unbiased and kind, wearing a long vintage Fiorucci yellow skirt with bright polka dots and a cut-off T-shirt with a bowl of pasta and the words Spaghetti Rocks on the front. My Docs, of course, gave it that London punk vibe.

Coming down the courtyard, I heard the sweet sound of Bobby's voice. "Yo, Charlie," he yelled from across the way, "what happened to your stomach?"

I sucked it in ASAP. "At least I can cover it, which is more than I can say for your *face!*"

He nodded. "Good one, man."

"Thanks, I thought so." I watched him leave and knew he'd be back. That kid, he just couldn't stay away for long.

Marta ran up behind me, pushing me aside in her typical psycho way. "Watch out!"

I almost couldn't look at her, but I did, and I swear it was an image that would not be leaving me anytime soon. "Oh my God, Marta, really?"

She'd teased her hair into a high, matted ponytail that defied gravity; the leotard she had on had to be her grandma's. All the elastic was gone, and it hung so low on her legs, she looked like she had on trunks. And the top was so stretched out that when she leaned down to read the lists, oh man—I looked away.

"What?" she snarled.

I shielded my eyes. "I can see your boobs, you know."

"I don't have boobs. They're nipples, and we all got 'em, so deal with it." She yanked open the door to the gym and disappeared.

I turned and saw Pen. She peeked in through the window. "So, who are you rooting for?"

The door opened. Fourth-, fifth-, and sixth-grade girls came running out, heads down, crying. They were all getting canned. They were thin enough but not good enough. Trixie would take the spot. Game over.

"Trixie, of course." I looked through the window. She was

up now, and I couldn't wait to see her perform. She looked amazing. "And Marta, but Marta for a whole other reason."

"Poor Marta," Pen said.

I opened the door and we went inside the gym. Trixie was already taking off her super sparkly silver warm-up outfit and walking onto the mat. I'm pretty sure she covered her body in silver glitter too, because everywhere you looked, Trixie glittered. Even her hair was sprayed with glitter. The crowd roared. "Go, Trixie!" I yelled as loud as I could.

"Go, Trixie!" Babette screamed louder from somewhere in the bleachers.

"Go, Trixie!" I took a deep breath and screamed as loud as I could. Ha! Take that, Babs! Just kidding, all right? I'm still on the path.

The room went quiet. Trixie was gorgeous. The sparkles glistened on her cheekbones, her lips were pink with gloss, and her eyelashes—put it this way, you could see them from where I was standing. And then she took off running.

I cringed a little. Even I saw the mistakes. But it didn't matter. Her cartwheels were flawless; her backflip caught major air. She was still amazing. When she completed her floor routine, the room went nuts.

Lillian, aka Ms. Fancy Pants Team Captain, was on the microphone before Trixie could catch her breath. "Ladies and gentlemen, was that fantastic?"

They roared. Trix ran into the huddle. They all wrapped

their arms around her like it was a done deal. I turned around and saw Marta on the sidelines looking like she wanted to kill someone. Trixie threw me a thumbs-up. I threw one right back at her.

And then Marta walked down the mat, under the spotlights. And everyone stared. They covered their mouths like they were witnessing a crime scene; they gossiped, turned away. I know what they were all thinking—how could any mother let her kid out like that? It was worse than child abuse.

"Marta Urloff's up. Marta's in seventh grade. This is her first time trying out for the team. Marta, come on up!" The crowd went crazy but not in a good way—laughter, boos, screeches. I knew it would be painful; I just hoped it'd be quick. Marta was standing there on the giant mat. Her stained, faded leotard—I'm guessing the same one she wore last year—flapped against her muscular bluish-white legs. Her arms up high, her face focused on nothing and everything. Lillian and her gang were giggling and gossiping, of course, tapping and rolling their eyes at poor Marta's delusion.

I closed my eyes, held on to my beads, and said a silent prayer that her humiliation would be quick.

"Marta Urloff, it's now or never." The announcer tapped the microphone; he paused, then added, "Earth to Marta."

The entire room exploded into laughter. I covered my eyes and peeked. But then Marta did something that made the whole room go quiet. With her arms bent in a ridiculously backward position, she ran down the mat and did the highest, most flawless round-off back handspring into an almost impossible backflip. I dropped my hands from my face. It wasn't possible; I must have dreamed it.

Everyone was dead silent, all eyes on her. No one spoke. No one. Marta just stood, breathing heavily in the silence, staring back at them all with the look of a champion who could not be squashed. Then, as though it was an afterthought, Marta bounced on the springboard and landed on the beam with the ease of someone who'd been magically placed there. We all watched as Marta the Farta executed a perfect cartwheel, like a slow windmill, that fell into a series of perfect somersaults and into a double-back dismount. She landed on both feet, flat and still. The room inhaled—you could feel it, the collective anxiety, disbelief, and, yes, excitement. Her hands flew up; her chest went out; her eyes pointed at the heavens. The room was speechless.

"Oh. My. God." Pen's brain was still trying to make sense of it all. She turned to me. "Did you know?"

My mouth still would not close. "Are you kidding me?" I watched Marta walk off the mat in the complete silence. People could not reconcile it. How? How could someone so homely, so uncoordinated and angry at the world, fly so high, be so powerful, so precise, and, yes, so beautiful?

"She's gonna get it, for sure." Pen smiled. "She's incredible; she's going all the way."

"All the way," I mumbled.

Coach got up quickly and walked over to Captain Lillian. Something big was going down. The air was hot with sweat and bad breath; people were on the edges of their seats. I caught Felix up in the top row, sitting with his whole class, waving at me. I did a little wave back.

Coach was turning red, but Lillian wasn't backing down. She had her hand over the microphone; her face was in his giant, hairy ear. He was shaking his head. She turned to look at her teammates, and at Trixie, and you could tell they'd rather cut out their tongues than admit that Marta was better than they'd ever be. Finally Lillian had the last word, and with my rudimentary lip-reading abilities, I was able to pick up something along the lines of *If you don't give Trixie another chance, we're all gonna walk, and you'll have no team. Got it?* Then the coach looked down and stormed out.

Lillian returned to the mat, microphone in hand, smiles all around. "Thank you, Marta, but there are many factors that go into being on the team." She shrugged, gave her that sad-dog look, like she was about to totally can her.

Somewhere in the crowd, someone started to boo. Marta paced, arms crossed over her chest, head down, waiting for it.

And then you'd never believe what happened. The door flew open, and Coach walked back into the auditorium and kissed Marta twice on the cheeks, Euro-style. He announced to the crowds, "On Friday we come back and have deciding round."

He looked at Trixie. "You have one week to train. Train hard."

Trixie went white. She knew what that meant. Everyone knew what it meant. Coach had given her another chance. "Marta, Marta, Marta," the crowd chanted.

I looked over at Pen, and she nodded. There was something so deliciously fair, so wonderful about all of this. In minutes Marta had gone from the most hated to the most loved. Wow, only in America can we make our villains into heroes so dang fast.

Trixie came up to me, head down like she wanted to run away as fast as she could. "Let's go," she said, her voice cracked and shaken.

I wanted to, but— "Where's Babs?"

"I don't know and I don't care. Come on," she said.

I looked around for Marta but couldn't see her anywhere. "Sure." We pushed the doors open and walked into the warm canyon air.

The Evil Plot

We walked all the way up Wonderland Park Avenue huffing and puffing in silence. A couple of times I looked over and could see that Trixie was in a state of total shock. At the stop sign, just before we were to turn off, Trixie finally stopped, put her hands on her hips, and paced in a small, tight circle.

"Unfrickinbelievable!" She grabbed her ponytail and yanked out the elastic. "How is that even possible? How can she be that good? Does she have a twin? Did she hire a look-alike? It's just not possible. I've known her for a year, and not once, not once, have I seen her so much as stretch. You've seen her, right?"

"Yeah, I have, she's totally—"

"Uncoordinated. Incapable, a spaz, a freak, nasty, dirty." Trix was going nuts; she could not stop rambling.

I waited until she was out of breath. "I guess she's been training."

Trixie stopped cold. "She's better than I am. My life is over. Over. You have no idea what this means. My parents were going to come to all the meets." She paced, looking a little nutty. "They never go to anything I do. My housekeeper does. And now she's gonna get my spot, that freak, Marta the Farta!"

"But you fit in," I shot back. "You look right; you look better than right. You look fantastic, and that's sometimes just as important."

She looked up. "That's true. A team's a team."

"And as much as it pains me to say this, they won't accept her," I said sadly. "They can't trust her; she's a loose cannon in need of some pretty major therapy."

"You just could be right." Trixie was thinking it over. "And if Marta looks and acts the way she does," Trixie said, looking hopeful, "then I might just have a shot."

"Good. Now"—I took Trixie's backpack—"let's get you home." We followed the road around the bend, past the house with a drawbridge, until we got to her huge fortress of a house.

While her parents worked away shrinking other people's brains, Esmerelda was there with brownies and milk, which we took into Trixie's room. She fell on her bed and stared up at the ceiling. She rolled over. She blew her nose and looked at me. "How am I going to tell them?"

"Come on, Trix, you haven't lost yet!" I searched through

her gymnastics movies until I found *Stick It*—her all-time favorite. I handed her the remote control. "Practice like crazy; watch all your practice tapes; get it down to a science. You do have a serious shot," I repeated. "You do." She blew her nose harder. Truth was, if it was based on skill and talent alone, she didn't have a prayer in you-know-what.

The phone rang; Trix scanned the caller ID. "It's Babs— hold on." She picked it up, listened in total silence, and then let out a massive scream. "You did what? No way! Where?"

I was listening, watching her face, totally trying to decipher what the heck was going on. Whatever it was, it was big.

Trixie got up and paced. "Come on, the principal would totally know, wouldn't he?"

She was *not* crying anymore. She even looked happy. I was feeling the old, familiar tingle of jealousy. "What?" I tried to get her attention. "What's going on?"

She turned, covering the phone with her hand. "Babs followed Marta today after the tryouts, and guess what?"

"What?"

"She got on a bus! A bus!" She tried to stop smiling. "She might not even live in our school district, which would disqualify her from the team, because by law she's not even supposed to be going to Happy Canyon. Can you believe the luck!"

Apparently Trixie's parents had single-handedly founded the Committee of the Canyon, and they loved kicking people out who didn't live here. Since when was public school such a hot ticket? All my life I envied the girls going to private schools in limos, crossing through those gates that locked the second their car pulled in, those rolling green lawns, security guards to keep all the paparazzi from finding them. Trixie quickly explained that Happy Canyon was hot, hot, hot right now for the following reasons:

1. A lot of celebrities were super cheap and sent their kids there instead of to the obscenely expensive private schools down the road, where they belonged.
2. Principal Pickler loved celebrities and would do anything to get them to come to his school and pose for lots of pictures, so that he could piss off other principals and win the Coolest Public School in LA award.

Trixie's eyes got all conniving, and she wagged her long finger that had a pretty scary-looking fingernail on it. "I swear I'm so gonna tell my parents to do a sweep."

"A sweep?" I looked at her.

Trixie threw up her hands like I was seriously dumb. "It's when they send people to go check addresses to make sure people are really living there. So many of them give fake ones, or places they don't live in anymore, it's criminal."

"Oh, come on." I thought of poor Marta.

But Trix shook with the thrill of it all. "Nationals, here I come!"

I got up, tapped her on the shoulder, and said, "Stop, Trix, stop, stop."

Trix turned, glaring at me. "Why?"

"You can't get her kicked out *now*; seriously, think about it."

"What's to think about?" She shrugged. "My parents are heads of the committee. This is what they do."

"Right." I nodded. "But before you and Marta compete for the team?" I shook my head. "Seriously, how's that gonna look to everyone, huh, Coach included?"

Trixie dropped the phone to her chest. She closed her eyes. "You're right—it'll look like I'm doing it to get her disqualified."

And then I added, "Yep, like you're not good enough."

"You are so right." She picked up the phone and began talking.

I fell back on her bed, stared up at the ceiling, and closed my eyes, bullet dodged.

"Change of plans," Trixie said. "No one can think we're trying to get Marta booted." Long pause while she listened and paced. I was just about to slip into a delicious only-child dream when I heard, "That's why I'm sending Charlie."

I bolted out of bed. "What?" I watched her hang up the phone and slip into a bathing suit. "You're sending me where?"

"To find out whether it's true or not. See, Babs didn't actually follow her home; Marta ditched her." Trixie combed her hair. "She's got something to hide, I know it—"

I cut in. "Trixie."

"Don't worry," she said, stopping me. "I'll wait until the

competition's over, and then we'll tell my parents. It's my duty, you know that, right?"

"Yeah, I guess," I said, but I didn't. Not anymore. She had no idea what it felt like to get kicked out of school.

She sat down on the edge of the bed, looking up at me with those baby-blue eyes. "You want me to win, right?"

"Of course I do." I kinda melted.

She touched my knee. "Then you'll help me?" she asked. "I'd help you. You know that, right?"

"Yeah," I said, looking at her, ever careful. "Of course."

"I knew you would. Here, try one of these." She pulled open drawers and tossed a billion bathing suits onto the bed. "You'll look beautiful in this one." She picked up a great polka-dotted red-and-white bikini. And then we rode the elevator and pretended like we were just a couple of nice girls. But we weren't.

Attack of the Hairy Teen

When I got home, Pen was nibbling on carrots, super annoying in and of itself. Who the heck eats carrots when there are tubs of buttercream frosting begging for a spoon? When she saw me, she stopped talking to Mom and got all up in my grill. "That was seriously uncool what happened to that girl today, and you were supporting the *wrong* choice."

I took a deep breath. "First of all, hello, Pen, Mom. It's nice to be home. And secondly, Pen, I was supporting both of them."

"You are such a liar." She crossed her bony legs and picked up an apple. "You want Trixie to win because you like her more, but Marta—oh my God! There's no comparison. It was so not fair."

"She was incredible, you're right, but"—I felt like a double agent, working for both Marta and Trix. "Gymnastics is a team sport."

"Made up of individuals," she said.

"Mom," I said, looking into the fridge, "tell her it's a team sport, please."

I sniffed. "What are you making?"

"Chili." She kept stirring. "It's a team sport, baby."

"And"—I had to cover my butt here—"if your teammate's farting all over you or doesn't wear deodorant or shave the pits, chances are you're not gonna want to spot her." I paused for effect. "Am I right?"

"Sad but true." Mom nodded.

"Now let's add to this the fact that she's on the team illegally—would that build unity?"

Pen stopped crunching. "Why illegally?"

"According to Trixie, looks like Marta doesn't even live in our school district, which means she has no right to be in our school, or on the team."

Pen was taken aback by this one. "Really? How is that even possible?"

I poured myself a tall glass of lemonade and found a bag of Doritos. Mom gave me this look, and I gave it right back to her. "I'm only having a few, all right? Plus I had no breakfast."

Pen started shaking her head. "Trixie's a real piece of work."

Let me pause for a moment and reflect upon Doritos. Eating them just had to be the most incredible experience in a lifetime. I wished everyone would go away so I could close my eyes and eat the entire bag without distraction.

"If Trixie's trying to get her kicked out," she started, strutting around the kitchen like a peacock, "I swear to God, I'll go to the principal myself and tell him why—"

"Jeez, she's not trying to!" I lied, of course. If Trixie lost, she'd do everything in her power to get Marta kicked out, including blackmailing me. "Take a break from saving the world and eating carrots. Have a chip, all right? She's not doing anything to her. She wants to win fair and square." Which was true. "You really should give her more credit."

"Trixie shouldn't even be getting a second chance at this at all," Pen stated matter-of-factly. "Marta's a better gymnast, plain and simple, better than anyone on that team."

Oh God, I located one of the orangest chips, caked with that all-American perfect Dorito seasoning. It melted on my tongue. I needed another moment of reflection. Oh, heaven on earth, thy name is *Dorito*.

"Sometimes, Charlie, you have to take a stand." Pen shook her head in disgust. She walked up the stairs. "I gotta go correct papers."

Stand? Give me a break. It was the weekend. I leaned back and had another chip. "Hey, Mom, can Trixie and Babs come over tomorrow and dig for tunnels?"

"Of course, my sweet baby." Then she picked up the bag of chips I was eating *while* my hand was still in the bag and walked away. Jeez, zero respect, huh?

Closing In on Houdini

Supposedly, Houdini wrote down everything in his journals, which he kept locked in his famous leather trunk. Everyone, and I mean everyone, looked for it after he died, but it had never been found. But I knew where it was. No doubt about it. It was hidden in the tunnels.

Anyway, one afternoon in the middle of summer, on one of those rare days my parents let me out of my cage, I was up by my Houdini statue when I saw a piece of trash sticking out of the dirt. But it wasn't trash; it was an old hand-drawn map of the tunnels that someone had buried, and had it not been for the gopher that'd been digging holes, I don't think it would have ever been found.

It stank like super bad body odor, so at first I thought it was a pair of Penelope's underwear. But it was actually a map of the whole place above and beneath the ground before it all burned down. I'd read it so many times. My dad and I did everything we could, and still we could not locate the tunnels. So I thought maybe Babs and Trix could shed a little light.

"Oh my God, look at this!" Babette stared at the map, more excited than I'd ever seen her. "Is it possible? An elevator, tunnels, all right under us?"

According to some people, Houdini's wife closed off the tunnels when she discovered he was having way too much fun over there.

"Looks like if we dig here, we'll hit the tunnels, right?" I shook my head. "But they're not there. We've gone over this spot a thousand times."

Trix was shaking her head. "What if it's not far down at all? What if the entrance is right on the surface, like a trapdoor?"

I couldn't believe she got there so fast. "You know, that's exactly what I'd been thinking."

Then she said, "And what if you've been reading it left to right all this time?"

I stared. "What?"

"Instead of right to left." She crossed her arms like a super cool fashionable explorer. "People who made maps always did things like that to confuse you."

"They did not!" Babs laughed, and Trixie kicked her.

But me, I studied. There was a spot that looked like an X that I had always assumed before was a cross. "No, it can't be,"

I said, and yet the more I looked at it, the more it was possible. "Right to left—let's give it a shot." I grabbed her and hugged her. We jumped up and down.

Trix was so excited, she hadn't mentioned gymnastics or Marta once. "What if it's full of dead people?"

Or the dead animals Houdini was trying to make disappear, like he did to Jennie the elephant. The greatest trick ever, making an elephant disappear from the stage just like that.

"Yeah! Let's get the shovels." I rolled up the map and ran for my dad's shed. "Dead people and animals, here we come." Babette, Trixie, and I started digging. We thought we could hit the trapdoor that afternoon, crawl down the steps, and come face-to-face with all of Houdini's secrets, but sadly, in life, I have found that everything *takes way too long*.

We quit after an hour. "This is going to look amazing for Halloween." Babs checked out all the seriously cool decorating work Mom had done.

"So who exactly are you inviting?" Trix went to wash off her hands in the natural spring, then saw a carving of Houdini underwater and got spooked. "Can I use the kitchen?"

We walked in, and Mom, my great mom, was making brownies for us. Pen was perched on the counter ready to eavesdrop and judge, her two favorite hobbies. "Thanks, Mom." I grabbed a seat and started eating while Trix and Babs were still washing.

Trixie picked up a brownie, took a bite, and almost had a

heart attack. "OMG! What did you put in these brownies?"

"It's just a mix," Mom said.

"Simply the best brownies I have ever eaten in my life."

RED ALERT: Never, and I repeat, never go for the You Are the Best Cook Ever routine with a parent. They see through it and know you are evil.

Mom caught on right away. "I'm happy you like them," she said in a kinda mean voice. Pen rolled her eyes. I could so see what was happening, and it was not good. They were ganging up on my friend in silence. "We're inviting everyone," I announced proudly. "Everyone in the entire class."

"I so love when people do that. It's just good karma, right?" Trix licked her lips and glanced at Mom.

"Speaking of good karma, any news on Marta?" Babs gulped milk down, totally oblivious of the fact that this was not the time or the place to talk sabotage.

I checked to make sure Mom didn't hear it. "I haven't had time yet."

Trixie took a tiny sip and stared straight at me. "You should go, like now."

"Go where?" Pen asked.

I glared at her. "Nowhere. Go away, Pen."

Trix batted her lashes. "Nowhere, Pen."

"I thought we were going to wait," I said, lowering my voice and my head. Pen could read lips, you know. "Until after the competition."

"Change of plans. We're gonna need to find out now," Trixie whispered. "Now."

Pen grabbed an apple and walked past. "Even if she lives outside the school district, she could still have a permit, you know."

"Pen!" I yelled. "Stop listening to our conversation!"

Mom put down more brownies, checked our glasses, acting like this was a totally normal conversation to have. "Like work, siblings, transportation, you name it." She poured more milk. "There's a permit for it. You'd better check on it before you get yourself into trouble."

"Oh, I wasn't going to tell!" Suddenly Trix was playing the dumb blonde. "Of course she could have a permit, and I sincerely hope she does, Mrs. C." Trix got up and walked around the table until she stopped right behind me. "But even if she doesn't, I won't say a word until after the competition."

Babs shook her head. "Not a word, Mrs. C."

Trix looked at Babs. "It would look bad and underhanded, and I don't want that." She batted her eyes at my mom and picked up her Gucci purse, like she was ready to go.

"No," Mom said tightly, "you don't."

"And anyway"—Trix came over and put her arm around me—"my good friend Charlie already warned me to keep my mouth shut, and she is right." She shrugged. "My lips are sealed."

"Yeah, sealed," Babs agreed. "Thanks, Mrs. Cooper."

Mom gave them a dirty look. And Pen, she watched them leave like they were a pack of yipping hyenas dragging off a deer. I got up and followed them to the door, feeling hopeful that maybe, just maybe, this whole thing would be put to rest until after the competition. "See you on Monday, guys."

But the second they were out the door, Trixie pulled me close and whispered in my ear, "Find out where exactly she lives. No matter what. I want to know by Monday."

"Ah, come on!" I said tiredly. "You promised to wait."

"Monday." And then she was gone, Babs trailing after her.

After they left, there was silence in the kitchen. I was just about to go take a nap when Pen announced, "You have to go to Marta and warn her right now! Right this very moment."

"Oh, come on!" I grabbed another brownie. "It's Saturday. I'm mentally exhausted; I have to think." My bed was calling me:

Charlie

Charlie

Charlie

"Find her address," Mom instructed, "and then go warn her. If it's true, it'll give her parents time to apply for a permit, or at least ask Principal Pickler or Coach for special permission. There's no telling what those girls will do," Mom said, "especially the little round one who's so eager to please that know-it-all."

"Babs." Pen shook her head. "She's just a victim."

"Great." I glared at Pen, thinking how I wanted to make *her* a victim. Of a bloody crime committed by yours truly.

My Mission of Good Hope

It took me, and I'm not bragging here, all of three minutes to find Marta's real address. So the next day, Sunday, my day off, I hopped on the very same little neighborhood shuttle bus that apparently Marta the Farta took every day to and from school. The doors shut. I looked out the window and watched my house fade away into the distance.

TRUE FACT: Mom was not worried at all about me taking the bus all alone. Is she mean or what?

But Marta's couldn't be too far. After all, she did this twice a day, every day. But the bus just kept on going up and up through the canyon, over the top of Mulholland and down into the valley, for such a very, very long time. It turned this way and that, until suddenly I realized I had no idea where I was going. All I knew was that I couldn't get off until I heard the words *End of the line*. That was her stop; you couldn't miss it, the bus driver said.

When we left the nice canyon and dropped into the hot valley, the bus got packed. That's when I closed my eyes so that all the old people with all their bags of veggies would stop trying to take my seat. I figured if they thought I was sleeping, they'd leave me in peace.

Anyway, when I woke up, we were smack in the slums. The bus was nearly empty. "End of the line," the bus driver bellowed, and we all walked off like a row of inmates.

We stepped out into the hot, hot sun. Jeez, where the heck were we, and how was I ever gonna get home again? With shaky hands I took out my directions and followed them. *Take a right, then first left, then another right. 2346 Reseda Avenue.* The busy streets soon fell away to small neighborhoods with tiny row houses. And then I saw it. A brown house with brown roses. An old orange Pacer sat in the garage under a thick blanket of dust.

I went up the driveway and knocked on the door. I knocked again. Feet came pounding, hard and mad. For a second I wanted to hide behind the car.

Marta yanked open the door, screaming at me before she even knew who it was. "What do you want?" She was in the same stretched leotard; her face was red, veins were bright blue under her skin, and she was sweating everywhere. Super gross.

I stared at her. I did not want this to be the case. It complicated my life to no end. "Oh God," I said, almost collapsing. "Please, please, don't tell me you actually live here."

She was just about to slam the door in my face when I stuck my fantastic electric-blue Dr. Marten in. And guess what? She still slammed the door as hard as she could on my foot without even flinching.

"*Oooooowwwww!!!!*" I checked my boot. "Man, you're really mean."

"Get lost!" She walked away, leaving the door wide open, and that, ladies and gentlemen, was when I should have just walked away and given Trixie the address. Wow, my life would have been a whole lot easier. Think about it:

Marta would have gotten kicked out, and then I'd be done, *done*! I'd tell Dr. Scales the truth, blame it all on Trixie, of course, and *bam*! I'd be set free from the mental-health institution.

But God help me, I felt sorry for her. She just seemed so alone. Even though, for all I knew, she could have had a *huge* family in there, she seemed so alone.

I watched Marta storm through the house, her back covered in tight, tiny, ripped muscles, muscles I never knew existed.

I followed her. Inside, it was cool, as dark as a cave, with brown, plush carpeting so thick and squishy your poor shoe disappeared when you walked. On the mantel of their old brick fireplace, I spied a photograph of a very small woman with Marta's eyes and the same dead gray complexion standing on a podium and wearing a red-and-white leotard and a silver medal around her neck.

I got closer, picked it up, and studied the heck out of the old photo. No way, no way. But they looked identical, and not in a good way, if you get my drift. Could it be true? Marta's mom, an Olympic medalist? And they lived in this dump? That was when the glass door to the garden slid open. I spied uneven bars, mats, rings; you name it, it was there. And so was Marta. She was headed right for me, her leotard stretched long and low, steam comin' out of her ears, veins popping—

"Put that down!"

"Whoa, whoa, I'm here to help, all right." I looked at the photograph in my hand. "Is this your mother?" She ripped it from me and carefully put it back in its place, on its dusty shrine.

Man, her mother might have been a good gymnast, but she was a horrible housekeeper and not too hot in the fashion or hygiene departments, either.

Marta was a mess. A wreck. Her hair was more than just not combed. It looked like it had *never* been combed. Her teeth were yellow; her nails long and jagged; her clothes looked like the pile the Salvation Army said *no* to.

And she was violent. She pushed me backward until I slammed into the wall. Her voice dropped low like a guy's. "What did they offer you to get rid of me?"

"Offer, what offer?" Was that spinach in her teeth? "Dude, I just came to warn you that some people know you live out of district, that's all."

"Who's 'some people'?" She laughed. "Trixie? Babette? Lillian?"

She went to the desk in the entranceway, took out a rather official-looking sheet of paper in a plastic sleeve, and threw it at me. "Here!" On it was written Permit to Transfer and then a whole bunch of boring stuff in fine print. "I'm allowed to go to Happy Canyon, so you can tell Trixie that she'd better start practicing." Marta stood over my shoulder breathing like some weird crazy person. "Now get the hell out of here."

I was just about to hand it back to her when something caught my eye. A number. "Oh, crap." I read it again. "It's expired." I nodded. "This September."

Marta's face went white. "What?" She pulled the permit from my hand and read it and reread it. "Oh no! You're lying. This can't be possible!"

"Well, where's your mom?" I said calmly. "You can get this fixed by next week, no problem."

The vein that ran down the middle of her forehead popped out again. "I said none of your business!"

"I'm just saying, it's not too hard. She just has to renew the permit, that's all." I stopped; Marta was in full panic mode.

Her hands balled into fists. "Get out!"

"Okay, okay."

I backed down the driveway and ran to the bus stop.

Trixie's Freaking Out Big-Time

When I walked through my front door and saw Felix sitting there playing with his thing-a-ling again, I just smiled. Then I hugged Mom. I was so grateful to be home.

"Hey, baby." Mom smiled at me. "So how far was it?"

"You have no idea."

"That bad?" Mom rubbed my shoulders.

"That sad." I opened the fridge.

"I just cut some carrots," Mom said.

"Please, Mom. I'm depressed as it is."

"Mac and cheese?"

"Now you're talking." I collapsed on the chair.

Pen came down the stairs in her shorts with her hair loose. Actually she didn't look half bad. Or maybe I was just dehydrated.

"I'm guessing she doesn't live in the neighborhood."

"You could say that." I took Pen's glass of juice and drank it down.

"Thanks." She rolled her eyes and got up. "So she's illegal?"

"The good news is she's got a permit," I said.

Mom and Pen clapped. "Yeah! That's great news, baby!" said Mom.

"At least she has a semi-fair chance at winning now." Pen went to the stove, pulled out one of the noodles, and handed me the fork to see if the pasta was ready. I happened to be the expert noodle checker. "I'll give her a makeover if she'll let me."

"The bad news is," I said, nibbling, "it's expired."

"Okay." Mom put two heaping plates before us. "Her parents can renew it before the big showdown. It's Friday"—she shrugged—"plenty of time, thanks to you, Charlie."

"Yeah." Pen ate, all infused with the weird thrill she got from justice being served. "Had you not gone down there, she could have gotten booted out on a technicality."

I didn't have the heart to tell them that there was something else going on, something I really didn't understand myself. Why had Marta flipped out so badly, gotten so mad, so scared, when she saw the permit was expired? She acted like it was the end of the world. And where was her mom, and why didn't she dust or use her car? And even more pressing, what was I going to tell Trixie?

After lunch I called her. She didn't answer her cell, so I tried the house phone. I so wanted to get this over with, tell her the whole truth, but when her housekeeper answered with "Ms. Trixie went to Beverly Hills shopping with her mother," something in me flashed to poor old Marta in that depressing cave of darkness in the middle of nowhere.

"Thanks, Esmerelda. I'll call later." I fell back onto my bed and stared at the wall. I felt horrible. Last week, when I told Dr. Scales that I truly felt bad for Marta, he went into this whole lecture about middle kids being the most sensitive of all.

TRUE FACT: We're human sponges.

According to old Scaly Head, the older ones get all the attention, because they're the best at everything, like Penelope is. The younger ones rely on their looks. Hello??? Felix. But us? We're ignored. So when we see someone else in similar shoes, we feel it; we know it.

I picked up my reading assignment, oh my God, really! About some sad, poor English girl who wants to get married at twelve! *Boring.* I tossed it. Math integers! *Too easy.* Tossed it too. And then I read the news. Anything to take my mind off it, *but* the whole Marta picture would not leave my head. It just stayed there like a big, dark cloud. What was wrong with me? It was the beads; it had to be the beads. I took them off at once and put them in the box with the Mama T scarf and went out to dig some more in search of the tunnels.

Trixie called later that afternoon. She sounded so excited, it kinda made me sick. "So, how was she?"

"She's good." I took the phone and walked outside. I had the urge to go visit Mr. Houdini.

"Does she live out of district?"

I climbed up the hill. "If you call Reseda out of district, I'd say, yep, she does."

"Yes!" She sounded ecstatic. "That spot is mine."

It was getting darker outside, the mist moving in from the ocean like a curtain closing these warm canyons down for the night. I hiked up to the statue and looked at Houdini, felt his face. Trixie rambled justifications for turning her in now in my ear, reasons Marta could not go to school with us.

"Trix, Trix, hold on," I cut in.

"What? What?" she said, pouncing.

"She's got a permit." Dead silence. "Her mom's got a permit."

"What!" She yelled so hard into the phone, I could feel my eardrum pop. "How can that be? A permit? A permit for what?"

"A permit to go to Happy Canyon School." Dead silence. And then the explosion. "Are you crazy? Demented? How can she have a permit? What reason could she possibly have? Her mom doesn't work in the canyons, she's no celebrity, please. It's a lie. I swear to God, I'm going down there right now—"

"Not a good idea, remember?"

"But this has nothing to do with the team. If she's using an illegal permit, which I'm sure she's doing, Pickler has to know."

"But she's not. I saw it. I read it." I walked back to the house, went inside, kissed Dad on the cheek, and went up to my room. "Think about it. If you try to dig up dirt on her, they'll say you tried to get her kicked out because she was better than you. It'll backfire."

"But what if I'm right?" Trixie protested. "Huh?"

"Win first," I said, "then do your snooping. Do whatever you want." By then Marta would be 100 percent legal, and there'd be nothing Trixie could do to stop her. I'd make sure of that.

Mom called up, "Charlie? Dinner."

"I gotta go," I announced.

"Sure, sure," she said flatly, "you go."

Crap Hits the Fan

On Monday, when Mr. L read from *Huck Finn*, his voice was trancelike, his eyes almost closed, and he swayed like a creepy zombie.

"Listen to the language, the tone, the nuance. Can you hear it, do you hear it?" Then he started acting out all the different accents, and it was pretty scary. The class looked either mesmerized or horrified, I couldn't tell. I took the opportunity to slip Marta a note.

> Marta—
> Get that permit fixed and fast.
> She'll do anything to get the spot.
> Flush this note the second you can.

Marta slipped it into her pocket when she was done reading

and gave me a dirty look. Great, I thought, she was on top of it. I felt relief.

The bell rang; we all jumped up. I couldn't wait to get out of there. Felix's class was starting a vegetable garden, and I could think of no better place to open my lunch box and eat my chicken leg.

After snack Mr. L made us all put on deodorant. He even opened the windows.

"Open your language-arts text," he said, surveying the room, "and Charlie and Marta, please join us in our study of verbs."

Marta turned; she was ruffled. *The note, the note!* she mouthed, like I was an expert lip-reader. *It's gone.*

"What?"

Bobby kicked me under the table. "Pay attention, or he's gonna make us stay in."

"Fine!" I kicked him back.

"Verbs are simply wonderful little beings, so filled with life and light!" Mr. L turned from the board and smiled. "Motion, action, you feel it every time you utter a verb. Can you think of a verb, Trixie?"

"Oh, I can think of lots," she said with a smile. "Lie, steal, rob, trick, harm, cheat. Right, Marta?"

The next day Mr. L was going on again about how beautiful words were when the door opened suddenly. Principal Pickler stood in the doorway. I didn't catch any of this because I was asleep.

"Charlie Cooper," he called out in a not-so-nice voice.

Me, still sleeping.

"Charlie?" He looked closer.

Bobby kicked me hard under my desk. I jumped like a rocket.

"Ouch, you creep!" That was when I saw these giant legs in shiny, polyester pants. Principal Pickler was standing over my desk, looking down at me.

"What, what?"

"Come with me," he said.

"But I, I—" I stalled. This was not good.

He pointed at the mess at my feet. "And take your things."

Okay, that was seriously not good. That meant I was not coming back. The whole class was looking at me; there wasn't a sound in the room. Even the fish had stopped swimming. Mr. L put his hands over his face like he was an old lady at a funeral.

Walking down the long, empty hallways side by side with the principal was like seeing your own death about to happen but not being able to stop it. Vivid memories of the last time this very same thing happened came flooding back at me. Down the stairs, through the office. All eyes on me. He opened the door to his room; I stopped like I'd been shot.

Uh-oh.

Mom. Mom was sitting at his desk. Clearly I was in so much trouble. But what the heck did I do? For the first time in my entire life, I couldn't think of a single *major* thing I'd done wrong.

Mom turned. I could tell by the pinched facial muscles that she was beyond mad; we're talking in pain. *Pain.* Eyes red too. Oh Lord, this was it.

"Charlie," she said, "I'm ashamed. There's no other word for it."

I had no idea what she was talking about. Seriously. No idea. I'd been a model citizen to the point of nausea.

Pickler shook his head. "And to think we gave you a clean start, Charlie. The kind of malice it takes to do what you did—" He slapped the desk. "It's just spiteful, mean, indicative of serious criminal propensities."

"Wait, wait," I cut in, "what the hell—" And then I saw the crucifix on the desk. *Hell* was not a good choice of word. "I meant crap, not hell, wait, which is worse?" I looked over at Mom, who was covering her face with a pretty floral scarf.

Pickler stood up, rolled up his shirtsleeves, and put his big plastic shoe on his chair. "Charlie, she may not be a fashion model like you, but Marta is a valuable part of our school."

Was I detecting a little sarcasm?

"For you to take the trouble to do this"—he held up an

envelope—"makes me think you're not a good person."

On his wall were framed pictures of him with every celebrity he could get his hands on. He took out the letter he was accusing me of writing. I stared at it, like it was some joke. "You think I did that?" It had all those cutout, creepy newspaper letters tipping off the principal that one Marta the Farta lived in Reseda, address included. Signed Charlie Cooper. They left out the C, of course. Because it was not *me*!

Mom began ranting. "Charlie, how could you? I thought you cared about Marta?" She was aging by the second. "We were all so sure you'd changed."

"Wait." I had to take a moment to really comprehend that they'd think I was so totally unoriginal. "You honestly think I'd leave my name?" I looked at Pickler. "Please, how dumb do you think I am?"

Pickler nodded brightly. "Clearly you think you're doing us a favor by reporting on a student coming to this school illegally, but, young lady, we are not living in the 1950s when students turn each other in. She doesn't even know about this; it came directly to me." He grinned. "So your little plan failed. It's like it never happened."

I looked at them both, shocked. "But I didn't do it. I'd never do something like this."

"And let me tell you"—spit was collecting in his mouth—"even if it were true, I wouldn't expel her on principle. You got that?"

I nodded. "Nice play on words, dude."

"Thank you," he chirped, "and don't call me 'dude.'"

Mom cut in, her hands wringing her purse strap in her hands. "Was it the pressure? Did they force you to do it? Did *she* force you?"

"Force you?" Pickler shook his head. "Who's forcing who?"

"No one is forcing anyone. No one can force anyone." I glared at Mom, hoping she'd shut up.

"Tell him," Mom commanded.

Pickler touched Mom's arm, nodding like it was his turn now to give me a thrashing. "We have a policy here at Happy Canyon: Students who attempt to better themselves at the cost of another student are automatically suspended and face disciplinary action."

Mom jumped out of her chair. "Charlie, tell him!"

The injustice of it was sickening.

The phone was ringing off the hook, but Pickler didn't even look; he was enjoying this too much. "Tell me what?"

Nope, no way.

Mom elbowed me. "Charlie, you're going to be suspended. Tell him!"

"You're barking up the wrong tree, Pickler. It ain't me, but I ain't no snitch neither."

"Fine. Have it your way." Pickler narrowed his eyes, pounded the desk. "Suspended until I get a full report from

Dr. Scales." He gave me this look of grave disappointment. "Mark my words"—his eyes bugged out—"never, never will I allow what happened at Malibu Charter to happen here."

Mom got up. "Come on, Charlie."

"Where are we going?"

"Guess." She grabbed me.

Pickler folded his arms and studied us. "I won't let her back in without a full evaluation." He made a point of looking at his gallery of framed celebrity photographs. "I have a lot of very important families here, you know?"

"I didn't do it," I said, but he just gave me a smirk like he didn't care what I had to say at all.

TRUE FACT: Grown-ups don't want you to change. It's so much easier for them if you stay the same.

I knew where we were going. Didn't even have to ask. We headed south down Laurel Canyon and swung a right onto Sunset Boulevard, where the resident homeless guy waved his dumb flag. I bet he wasn't falsely accused on a daily basis like yours truly.

When Scales saw me, he shook his head for a seriously long time, like I could have watched an entire episode of *Cake Wars* and he'd still be nodding. "So tell me, Charlie, why did your principal, whom I know and respect—"

"Really?" I had to cut in here. "You know him, *and* you still respect him?" Mom elbowed me.

Dr. Scales looked seriously disappointed. He leaned back in his chair, putting his hands in front of his face like he was tired and all out of tricks. "What did you do, Charlie?" He blew out a lot of hot air. "You were on such a good path; we've worked so hard—"

"Doc, stop," I said, his disappointment killing me. "I'm still on the path, Doc. I'm completely innocent, Doc, one hundred percent didn't do it."

He leaned forward. "Do what?"

I leaned even more forward; our faces were almost touching. "Set up Marta to get kicked out of school."

He fell back into his chair like he was seriously relieved. "So who did?"

"Ah!" I slapped the table. "If you'd all just let me out of here, I could take care of the whole mess."

Scales looked at Mom; Mom looked over at me. He said, "I really don't think she's responsible this time."

Say what? "Seriously, Doc?"

He wiped his lips with his hands, gross, and then he kinda chuckled like he was so smart. "Charlie would never sign her name on the note. She is not stupid."

"Maybe I'm so smart, I actually did sign my name because I knew you'd think I wouldn't. Ha!"

He shrugged. "See what I mean? Plus I'm quite sure Charlie has a conscience."

Mom gave him this weird look like she was totally not expecting that. "You are?" Then she looked down at me. "She does?"

I wanted to kick her. "Wow, thanks, Mom."

Doc put his hand on my shoulder. "So you got set up?"

"You're right on the money, Doc."

"So the question is why?" They both looked at me.

"Yeah, why, Charlie?" Mom folded her arms, her foot tapping.

Scales put his desk clock in his drawer. He shook his head. "I've got all afternoon."

I knew I wasn't getting out of here until I told them. "Trixie's using me to get Marta kicked out and is basically blackmailing me to keep my mouth shut."

"Trixie?" Mom's nose got all scrunched. "But she promised she'd wait until after the competition." She said it like she couldn't believe anyone but *me* would stoop to blackmail.

"She promised *you*," I said, "but *me* she sent to find out where Marta lived, and when I told her she had a permit, she still went ahead and wrote that letter."

"Why?" Mom tried to understand.

"She's stirring up trouble to see what she can find and blaming me for it." I shrugged. "As long as I take the fall, she can stir up whatever she likes."

"But Marta's getting it fixed, right?" Mom looked at me.

"Yeah, if she can," I said, and left it there.

That's when Scales got all up in my grill. "So, how are you going to handle this?"

"The way I see it, I've got three choices:

1. Let Trixie tell everyone at school the story of my downfall at Malibu Charter and eat alone until I graduate high school.
2. Shut up, do nothing, and let Marta get kicked out.
3. Make Trixie think I'm on her side; take care of Marta."

Dr. Scales thought for some time. "Which one is it?"

"Three." I announced. "It has to be three, right?"

Scales thought for a while, nodded.

"And I don't want you involved, okay? You promise me?" I was serious on this one. I mean, how can I ever be taken seriously if my shrink is getting all up in my business all the time?

Scales closed his eyes like he was falling asleep or dead. But then suddenly his eyes snapped open. "On one condition," he said.

I stared up at his hairy nostrils. "What?"

"If you get in over your head, call me."

"You have email?"

He jotted something down on the back of his card. "You are the only one I've given this to; use it when you need to."

Mom put her arm around me and smiled. "Will you tell the principal that you put her under truth serum, and she's innocent?"

"I'll call him now." He opened the door. "Good luck, Charlie."

"Thanks, Doc." The elevator door opened, Mom ran to get in, and so did I. I had some serious planning to do. I stared at the closed doors, not saying a thing.

It's Getting Hot in Here

I didn't go back to school right away. No way was I gonna walk into that classroom and have everyone turning around, whispering, staring.

Talk about post-traumatic stress.

So Mom took me out to lunch in Beverly Hills and ordered me a basket of chicken nuggets and fries with ranch, which was like my favorite thing in the entire world, but she *never* lets me eat it. On account of all those poor, skinny chickens that never see the light of day and have no feathers and grow old with all the hormones they're given. You know what, though? I really didn't care. As long as my nuggets were golden-crispy and came with fries and ranch, I couldn't care less where they lived before they made it onto my plate. Sorry.

"Here you are." The server put down the basket, and my

mouth began to water like crazy. I picked up a nugget and dipped it in ranch and chewed, waiting for the *zing* and the *zang* of all that meat and deep-fried breading to kick in, but there was nothing. Nothing! Flat. I picked up a fry, dipped it. "Oh my God!" I spat it out. "What the heck is this?"

Mom stabbed a piece of lettuce casually. "Oh," she said, "those are the sweet-potato fries; they're the new thing."

"Traitor!" I pushed them away.

She pointed. "And how about the nuggets?"

And then I got suspicious. "Um, why aren't you putting the word *chicken* in front of that?"

"Because they're made out of soy," she said, beaming. "Isn't that amazing?"

"And you're wondering why I need a shrink! The duplicity, the lies!" I stood up. "Take me to a McDonald's before I, before I—"

So she drove me to McDonald's, and I ate in the car like all good Americans do. On the way home, fighting our way up Laurel Canyon—no one respected an old Volvo—Mom asked me, "Charlie, are you getting yourself in too deep?"

It was a fair question, and it was one that had been bothering me too. I knew what Trixie was up to and how far she'd go to get what she wanted. I knew that she'd done her research on me and held my secret in her little hands. I could have said no and bowed out of this game altogether. But then I'd risk her letting it leak that it was me who got booted, shunned, and made to undergo major therapy, which would seriously hurt my street cred. I deserved a fresh start. So I had no choice but to play the game.

"I'll be okay, Mom." I put my hand on her shoulder. "It's different this time."

She glanced over at me with those mom eyes and then put her hand on the horn and honked until someone let us merge into the single lane that would bring us home.

When I got home, I took advantage of my snoring siblings' absence and stretched out for a long nap—digestion requires patience and care, people. When I woke up, I called Trixie and told her we had to talk about the Marta problem ASAP.

"Come over," she said.

"Sure, I'd love to," I lied, and hung up the phone. Man, I dreaded that walk. But in the name of duty, I put on my high-tops, and a pair of hip-hop sweats and told Mom I was going to deal with Trixie.

"Good luck, dear." She patted my back as I opened the door, covered my face, held my breath, and ran through the cloud of dust that covered our house now that they were digging an even larger crater in our front yard. Lucky for me, Dad wasn't there. If there was anyone who could tell that I was up to something, it was him.

I got to Trixie's house and rang the bell. Esmerelda answered and sent the elevator like I was a VIP. She met me with a snack and pointed to my shoes, which I removed promptly. I could hear a man's voice on the phone off in the study. His voice was smooth; even his laugh sounded like it came from a TV show. The door was open. I tried to get a look, but Esmerelda hurried me along.

"Come," she said, and I followed her to Trixie's room. She pushed open the door and, low and behold, there they were, Trixie and Babette, the two little schemers.

I wished my beads were on, because I was not feeling very kind at this particular moment. I stood there watching them giggle and gossip, so lost in their world, they didn't even notice I was there. They had fake champagne in real glasses and chocolate-covered strawberries on the bed, celebrating. Celebrating what? I wondered. My suspension or Marta's expulsion? "Hey, guys." I cleared my throat.

Trix jumped. "Charlie!" She put down her glass. "Finally!" She ran to me and threw her arms around me.

I picked up the bottle and drank straight from it, grabbing as many strawberries as I could and shoving them into my mouth, letting the juices run out. "I'm so sorry, Trix."

Trix stopped celebrating. "What do you mean?"

I collapsed onto the bed. The girls looked at me like I'd been struck with some kind of disease.

"So, so." Trixie shook me. "What happened?"

I sat up. "Pickler said, and I quote, 'Even if Marta lived in Romania, I still wouldn't kick her out.' Can you believe that? There's no way to get rid of Marta."

"That is unbelievable!" Babs covered her face.

Trixie turned purple. "Is that what he said?"

"Yep."

"We'll see about that." Trixie paced back and forth. "My mother always says, Where there's a will there's a way."

"Hold on a second," Babs said, like she'd just had the best idea ever. "When *was* the last time you actually saw *her* mother?"

"Wait, didn't she drive that weird corn car and wear socks and sandals?" Trix tied her long, beautiful hair up in a knot on the top of her head. "I totally remember her; she used to pick her up; we used to *see* her a lot."

"But not since last year." Babs smiled. "That was the last time we saw her. She didn't come to orientation, parents' night, or even the tryouts. So where the heck is Marta's mom?"

"You think she took off?" Trix asked. "Is that possible?"

Babs shrugged. "Just up and left her? Then who's taking care of her?"

Trix started tapping her desk with her long nails. "This year, I've never seen anyone, never. She's always alone."

"Think she died?" Babs looked at the two of us.

"Died?" Trixie's whole face went blank as she nodded. "And there's Marta—no dad, no relatives, can't go back to Romania, so she stays and pretends—"

"Come on!" I said. "No way! Her mom probably works two jobs; she's a single mom." I took a deep breath and felt worse

168

for Marta than ever before, like really bad. Like I didn't see the old, faded Disney outfits anymore or the hair or the food in her teeth. I just didn't want her to be living there alone. Who deserves that?

Esmerelda brought us a tray of cut fruit, and Trix pointed to her swimsuit. "We'll eat on the deck."

In the background I could still hear her father on the phone, still sounding like an actor. We got on the elevator. Trix's blue eyes got even bigger, and they locked in on me. "You're gonna have to go back and check it out."

"Me?" My stomach tightened. "Pickler already thinks I have it in for her."

Trixie suddenly looked like she cared. "That's exactly why you really need to run down there and see Marta's mom in person." The elevator opened onto the perfect heaven of a deck. Every chair had a thick, soft, white cushion on it; the sky was blue; there wasn't a single noise, a single moment out of place. I watched them walk out, and then the doors closed with me still inside. And, gladly, I left. I did not belong there.

Secret Door

I walked through the gate and saw Dad knee-deep in dirt, even his face covered in mud. Next to him was a small box overflowing with the earthworms he'd saved from being sliced in half with his shovel, 'cause that's the kinda guy he is. I ran to him, jumped in the hole, and hugged him as hard as I could.

"Whoa, whoa." Dad held me. "What happened?"

I let him hold me because I was exhausted. "I want to be like Jai."

Dad kind of laughed. "Why, because he doesn't go to school?"

"Yes, Dad!" I cried. "It's so hard, it's so hard." I wiped my nose on his sleeve. "Girls are so mean!"

Dad nodded. "We've really stuck you in a tough spot with this Marta thing."

I sat down in the mud pile; I didn't even care. All the beauty in my life was over. "Trixie's not my friend; she's on a mission," I said. "And she doesn't care who she steps on to get there. I always cared, you know. I did bad stuff, but I cared."

Dad nodded. "That's what makes you so lovable, Charlie." And then he got this crazy look. "I want to show you something."

I rubbed my eyes. "What's up?"

His voice was barely a whisper. "The door, Charlie. I think I hit the secret door."

"What!" My mind raced a mile a minute. "To Houdini's secret tunnels!" I could feel the door under my feet.

Dad got down on his hands and knees, feeling the square for a way in, and then he stopped and looked at me. In his hand was a padlock, a very old gold padlock. "It's locked. He locked it."

By "he," he meant Mr. Houdini himself. "Well, of course he locked it, Dad. This is where he's hidden his book of magic, the secrets to how he was able to escape from handcuffs and water jugs, and all the work he did on exposing fake mystics. This is the key to everything."

Dad beamed. "How do you know all this?"

"Oh my God, Dad, that was one of the coolest things about him. He was a magician, but he was totally against all those freaks who went around telling people they could speak with dead people."

Dad wiped his hands on a towel. "But I thought he thought *he* could talk to the dead?"

"No, never," I explained. "He was a scientist, Dad. His tricks were meticulously worked out; he didn't just appear on the scene, he knew *how* to get on the scene. Pretending to hear spirits was so not him." I stared at the trapdoor and could feel his world opening up beneath me, and you know what was so cool? It made mine feel so much smaller.

"I'll get my electric saw and tool kit!" Dad said. "I am so happy you're here with me."

"Me too, Dad." I waited for him to come back. It was hot; I felt like one of those worms with that nasty pink skin. In these tunnels Houdini practiced escaping from the most impossible places and devised his most famous illusions, like the time he made the elephant disappear.

Dad came running back, tripped over a rock, and picked himself up again. "I got it!" He held the electric saw, a great big grin across his face. The blade of his saw caught the sunlight. "We are about to make history." He turned it on and lowered it onto the thick-as-heck lock shackle, which turned bright orange; the blade cut through it; sparks flew everywhere. The lock fell off, and it was as big as his hand. He took off his glasses and smiled. Houdini's secret tunnels. Sweet! Dad lifted the cover. It smelled like a grave. "I can't believe it!"

I got closer, my heart pounding. "Let's go in."

Suddenly he backed off. "Maybe we should wait."

"Are you kidding me? Wait for what?" I was already thinking of charging admission.

"Maybe we should call Martin," he said. "He's the owner, you know. All this belongs to him, not to us."

"Dad, hello! Halloween is around the corner, Houdini's speaking to us, and it's not like we're going to steal anything!"

"I don't know, Charlie—" He shone his light inside. "We don't even know what's down there. Maybe black widows, snakes—"

Think I cared? No way. I jumped.

"No! Charlie!" he yelled after me. And then he jumped too, and fell hard on his backside, his flashlight and shovel making a horrible sound as they hit the rock. He shone the flashlight on the walls. There were pictures everywhere in silver frames and large, painted portraits of really ugly old people looking mean.

"Probably his in-laws," Dad said. They were one depressing bunch, serious and wrinkled, unpleasant. "Poor guy."

The air was cold and musty, but so far there were zero spiders, which I was secretly thankful for. I'd rather see a rat any day than a spider. We walked, our shoes making heavy sounds as we trespassed through this private sanctum. Mr. Houdini died on Halloween day in 1926. There were cold lanterns on the walls and carpets on the floor. It was like someone's house that had been left in a hurry.

But where was all the stuff? I'd had visions of it all summer long: In my dreams there'd be a stage; a thick, red velvet curtain hanging low to hide the giant steel milk can he submerged himself in so many times to figure out just how to contort his body, how to inhale and squeeze, how to get free. I'd find Houdini's trunk and it would be filled with secrets just waiting for me.

"Look at this place." Dad scanned the walls. There were lights made of copper; there were dangling chandeliers of cut crystal. "Imagine, this was where Houdini used to come up with all his magic acts."

I was just about to suggest I throw my Halloween party right here when we got to this circle area that looked like a living room, with red velvet sofas, a beaded lamp, and shelves of glass jars. "Cool. Dad, come here." And then I got closer. The jars were staring back at me. I grabbed Dad's arm, pointing. "Eyes!"

Dad put the shovel against the wall and scanned the shelf with his super bright light. "Look at this: dogs, cats, birds, reptiles," Dad said. "Our Mr. Houdini studied species."

I checked out the carefully labeled jars. "Why?"

"To see what happens to them under harsh circumstances. Like you said, he was a scientist." And then Dad stopped and made a face. He yanked my arm, hard. "You don't want to see this."

"What? What is it?"

"Nothing, baby, come on." Dad pulled. But you know that

just doesn't work for me, so of course I went right up to where he was standing. Skeletons were sitting on the sofa, a tea set before them. There was a door behind them and a large bookcase full of books.

Wow. "Are they real?"

"Think so." He took my hand and pulled me again, but I wanted to stay.

My brain flooded with some seriously cool decorating ideas. "Dad, I have to have my Halloween party down here, like absolutely have to." I was thinking, planning out loud. "We can make spaghetti and meatballs, Jell-O with spiders, Mr. and Mrs. Bones over there can—"

And that's when I heard the sound of my baby brother, Felix. *"Daaaaaad!"*

Dad looked torn. "Sorry, Charlie, I gotta get him. Your mom's working."

"Not a problem." I slapped him on the back. "I'll close it up."

He squeezed my hand. "You feeling better?"

"Are you kidding me? It's like a brand-new day." If Trixie opened her big mouth about Roxy, a party down here could turn me into a rock star at school.

TRUE FACT: Whenever you're stuck in a real bind, get lost in some other puzzle.

Pen, the Buzz-Killer

By dinnertime I'd all but forgotten about the huge mess I was in with Marta and Trixie. I felt calm and full of hope. I couldn't wait to get back into those tunnels and find what I knew was down there and then sell it all on eBay for a million bucks.

I looked up from my notes. "What if there's a secret chamber?"

Felix shook his head, clueless as usual. Pen had the same look.

"It's full of underground hot springs here." The more I thought about it, the more excited I was. "What if there's a chamber even farther down where he practiced his escapes and kept his journals—huh—journals that could be worth a fortune?"

Mom was at the stove, cooking what she'd called "mac and

cheese," but the longer it took, the more I suspected she was trying to hide vegetables in the mac and cheese. "You know, you might be right," she said. "The water flows from under this property across the street and all the way to the old Flynn property."

Felix got up and tried to take a look. "Are you hiding stuff in the mac and cheese, Mom?"

"Go away!" She swatted him, and we all sank a little lower, saddened and more than a little angry. We'd told her so many times that we could tell when she shoved some nasty vegetable into perfectly good pasta. We even threw away the cookbook teaching her which vegetables were the easiest to hide, but still she did it.

Pen tossed her napkin on the floor. "I hate when she does this."

"Tell me about it." Dad rolled his eyes.

"Yum, yum, yum!" Mom brought over the steaming pot of nastiness. I could smell the sweet potatoes before the pot even got to the table. I was devastated. Why ruin a wonderful dish? Why? She served us huge portions of it, but no one picked up their fork.

"So, baby," Mom said, eating it like it was gnocchi with *real* cheese, "what's happened with Trixie?"

I didn't really want to talk about it, because it just kept getting worse. "She says she's going to practice and win." I gagged.

"Don't believe it." Mom kept eating.

Dad raised his glass. "Let the best girl win." Then he took a bite of the fake mac and cheese and ran like he was covered in bugs.

Pen put her food in the compost can Pen had set up under the sink. It stank like you have no idea. "They'll find anything they can to disqualify her. That's just the way those kinds of people are."

Pen stood up, starting to pace the way she always did when she tried to solve an injustice. "This is what you have to do: Get her cleaned up; a new leotard would help." She went to her very own wallet, counted out forty big ones from the money she'd made tutoring kids at our old school, and handed them to me. Pen was rich, and worse, she was a hoarder. "I hate to condone this, but the only way for Marta to get a fair chance is to play their game, no matter how shocking it may be, so here."

I pocketed the cash. "You know it's easier to brush a lion's mane, Pen," I said tiredly, because you know what? I was tired. I just wanted to focus on Halloween, that's all. Instead I had to figure out how to get back to Reseda and risk being bitten, infected, and insulted one last time. Not to mention help her pick out leotards. But now it wasn't just for Marta; it was for me too. Sadly, our fates were linked.

The Pressure Is On, Big-Time

Before class started, Trix and Babs helped me hand out the invites to my Halloween party to my entire class. Yes, that's right, my *entire* class. Something I've never done before. Even Marta, God help me. I handed one to her, but at first she wouldn't take it.

"What's this?" She stared at it like it had been dipped in Black Death.

I slapped her hand with it. "An invitation to my Halloween party. Here."

Marta read it, stared at it, and turned it upside down like she'd never seen anything like it in her life. I caught her stuffing it in her shirt like a thief.

Trix came up behind me. I could feel her hot breath all over me, and it was seriously getting on my nerves. "*When* are you going over there?"

I reached over and handed an invitation to Bobby, and the way he checked out my faux leather motorcycle jacket I had picked up at this tight thrift shop on Melrose called Wasteland made the whole groveling to get the party worth it.

Trix never left my side. "We're running out of time."

"Her mom's gonna be there, Trixie," I said tightly. "She's not dead. Come on, be serious."

But she wasn't listening to me. "Around dinnertime or even later when her mom *has* to be home. Don't make me put the screws on."

I was like, What's that supposed to mean? But then Mr. Lawson came in. "Happy Tuesday morning to you, class." He opened his briefcase and took out a stack of papers. "Your essays." He walked the aisles dropping them on our desks. "The winner of the essay competition is"—he did a lame drumroll sound—"hands down, Marta Urloff!" He stopped at her desk. "Wow!" He grabbed his heart. "It was beautiful; you captured the death and sadness of the animal shelters like I've never seen it done before. It"—he looked all teary—"broke my heart, you know."

The rest of the class plugged their noses. That's what they always did whenever the teacher called her name. The jerks. Wait until she was standing up there with a giant hunk of gold around her neck, and they were all fat and watching it on their dumb TVs.

180

Later that afternoon, the time when most kids were out playing ball on their grassy lawns with their dads and their moms were cooking up a storm of cheesy delight for family dinner, I was standing on top of Marta's crunchy brown grass, looking at her brown house. And yet Marta was anything but brown. She may not have been the nicest person in the world, but she had a life force that was fierce.

TRUE FACT: I'm pretty sure Houdini was like that too. Maybe that was what you had to be like to really make it in this place.

I knocked on her door. Said a little chant I'd picked up on a self-realization website. *Let her mother answer, please, please, om, om, om . . .* The door swung open. Marta answered it in her standard dirty flappin' leotard and a scowl. "What do you want?" She stood, the late afternoon sun hitting her in the eye.

And so I began. "Last year I did something really stupid." I took a deep breath and kicked the grass; I didn't want to look at Marta. "I got kicked out for it. I lost all my friends; we had to move; they forced me to see a shrink. It was bad."

"So?" She shrugged, not interested at all.

"So we moved here for a clean start."

"Great, good for you." She was about to close the door when I stopped her.

"Trouble is, Marta," I said heavily, "there are no clean starts.

I'm pretty sure Trixie knows the whole story." I waited for some kind of recognition, some kind of realization of what I'd gotten myself into. But she said nothing. "And she's blackmailing me with it." Marta snorted. I took that as sympathy. "Yep, she's gonna tell everyone at school what I did unless I help her get you kicked out. That's all she wants, you out."

Marta nodded like a robot, like she was used to this kind of thing. "And now she and her parents are looking into my permit?"

"Yeah," but I could not say that they also believed her mother was dead, because somewhere deep inside me, I thought it could be true.

She leaned against the door like an old housewife. "All I want is to get out of here and never, ever look back. That's all." She turned, leaving the door open.

I followed after her. "I can help you."

"Why?" She snorted. "Why do you care? All you want is to be popular, to be *liked*. That's all."

"Why?" I shrugged. "Because I'm a half full kinda gal, Marta. That's why." I opened my bag, producing my framed diploma. "But I happen to hold my very own beauty-school certificate from an online salon based in the ultrafashionable city of Mumbai. I have my very own beauty dummy I have practiced on for a total of two hundred and fifty hours." And that's not counting what I do to Felix when he's crashed out.

Marta cocked her head. "What are you going on about?"

"Look, if you want on that team, you'd better stop training and start plucking, brushing, bleaching, and styling, because no matter how good you are, you're gonna scare the crap out of the audience." She didn't say anything. "I can help you win. I want you to win, not Trixie—"

But before I could even finish my sentence, she was gone. Then she was back again with long haircutting shears and a brush. She handed them to me. No one had ever given me scissors and begged me to cut their hair before. "All right, sit."

I studied her in the mirror. I felt a little woozy. I was seriously overwhelmed. Her hair was matted high above her head; her teeth were the color of sunny-side-up eggs (and we're not talking the whites); her skin was pale and freckly around her nose (good) but red and peeling all around her nostrils (not good). She had a mustache. And a unibrow. Again, not so good.

I took the brush and tried to get through her mop the way you would normally brush hair, but this was no normal hair. "Um, Marta." I yanked and pulled, but it wouldn't go through. "How long has it been since you brushed your hair?"

"I don't."

"Why?"

"Never thought about it until it started itching," she said, "and then it hurt too much." She shrugged.

I ripped and pulled knots out of her head, and Marta did not cry. Chunks fell to the ground. "I hope your mom has a vacuum cleaner."

"We do," she said tightly.

I pulled more. "So when does she get home?"

"Late." Even tighter.

I doused her with detangler spray from my bag.

"She works until closing," she added.

I pulled and I combed and I fished. "Where?"

"Bagel shop."

Bagel shop? An Olympic gymnast? *What?* "Why does she work at a bagel shop?"

"Why not?" She looked up at me all of a sudden, real mean. "You got something against bagels?"

I pushed her head down. "Are you kidding me! I love bagels!" I held her head down with one hand and ripped the heck out of her hair with the other. She was the toughest person I'd ever seen; didn't flinch, didn't give a single cry. "Did you know your hair's actually blond?"

"No, it's not—just give me a mirror, all right?"

"In a minute. Head down." I picked up the scissors and cut her hair straight across the neck. "Head up." I walked around in front of her. "Close your eyes." I took the huge chunk of mess that hung down, doused it with detangler, got the comb through it, and then I cut it off right below Marta's gangster unibrow.

She kept her eyes closed.

"Wait." I evened out the sides, went to the back, and made sure it was even too. I took some of my favorite pomade from my bag, and I ran it through, making her hair shiny and flat, unrecognizable. Beautiful. I handed her the mirror.

Her eyes lit up; she opened her mouth to say something, but nothing came out. She just stared at herself, repeating, "It's not me."

"May I present a perfect bob with bangs." Even I couldn't believe how good it looked.

Marta smiled at herself like she was a stranger, like she couldn't take her eyes off the mirror.

I looked at the clock; it was already five fifteen. "When your mom gets home, maybe we can borrow her tweezers and stuff, 'cause you got one nasty brow problem."

"Let's just do it now." She led me to the bathroom. "She won't mind."

She opened the cupboards, and they were full of beauty products, organized in straight rows. "She always had to be perfect for competitions." Marta touched her mom's stuff with delicate but shaky hands. "You can use it—just be careful with it, okay?"

I found the tweezers and positioned myself in front of her. "Close your eyes."

"Why?"

"'Cause this is gonna hurt like you-know-what." I grabbed a chunkful of brow hair, and I ripped out a row.

"Ouch!" Marta grabbed my wrist so hard, I felt her nails cutting my skin. "Stop it now! This is torture."

Her skin was bright red where I'd ripped out the patch. I went for another hunk. "You want on the girls' team or the boys'?"

"Fine." She dropped my wrist. "Do it." I plucked and I ripped until the spot between her eyes was no longer a hedge. Then I got to work on her eyebrows and her chin. I told her to lie down.

She looked scared. "Why?"

I pointed to the carpeted spot between the toilet and the shower. "Just drop your head all the way back now."

She clenched her teeth. I had always fantasized about doing this to Pen while she slept. I stuck those tweezers in Marta's nose, and I ripped those hairs right out. Marta screamed, water sprang to her eyes, she cried, but God love her, she didn't move. "No wonder you have so many boogers; it's like a Venus flytrap in there with all that hair."

"It's the way Mother Nature intended."

"If Mother Nature had a mirror, believe me, she would have ripped this nose forest out with her bare hands."

Marta got up, her nose bright red, her eyes red with tears. She was about to leave when I threw up my leg. "Nope, now the teeth." Her shoulders sagged. "Did you know they're supposed to be white, not yellow?"

"American propaganda."

In her mom's stuff, there was like a year's supply of Crest Whitestrips. "Well, your mom sure knows it." Which bugged me, because if her mom knew it, why did her daughter's teeth look like corn? It just didn't jibe, right?

"Have to be white for competitions. Open up." I blanketed her fangs with bleaching strips. "Now these"—I turned to face her—"you have to wear these twice a day for as long as you can stand. Even if your gums start to melt, don't touch 'em, sleep with them."

Marta pulled her lip over the strips and got up. "Now I want to show you something." She walked across the living room and opened the sliding glass door. I followed her out into the walled square. All I wanted was for the dang door to fly open and her mom to walk through. That's it. Get permit fixed. Marta wins. Game over.

SPOILER ALERT: This was not meant to be.

The grass was covered with mats; in addition to the bars, there were rings, a beam, parallel bars, a vault, and a pommel bar. She walked around, touching all the pieces like they were art. "They were my mom's."

"I bet she practices here all the time," I said, hoping.

She took the rings in her hands and, within seconds, she was upside down, her body like a blade. I don't think I've ever seen anyone so good at something in my life. Then suddenly she was spinning round and round so fast, her new bob whipping around until she flew into a dismount, her back arched, her face pointed up to her patch of sky.

"Wow!" I clapped. She beamed. That's when I noticed the skin rash we still had to deal with.

I pushed her back into the bathroom. "Come on, time for some serious exfoliation." When I got the scrub from the shower, I saw all kinds of nasty rose shampoos, a sure sign of an old lady. "Sit." I opened the apricot scrub and removed at least a few layers of skin. I went for more; I went for pink.

She opened her eyes, and I noticed for the first time that they were a greenish brown. She closed them and got serious. "I'm the best gymnast in the school, but they don't want me on the team because they think I'm gross, that I'm ugly, even though I'd make them win." She was getting a little wound up; I could see the whitening strip move. Not good.

"Whatever you do, don't cry. We gotta take years of yellow off those teeth." I started to wipe off the mud mask I'd applied, and she closed her eyes and looked pretty peaceful. So I decided to ask what I'd been wanting to ask her all day, the question that would pretty much tell me everything I needed to know. "Marta, did your mom get your permit renewed?"

She started to cry. "Am I done?"

TRUE FACT: I pretended not to notice. Remember how I told you middle children absorb everyone's problems? Today I really didn't want to be a sponge.

188

"Yep." I rinsed, moisturized, applied some of her mom's light foundation, mascara, and lipstick, and brushed her silky hair. "I think you're done."

Marta got up and looked at herself in the mirror. Slowly her chest began to heave, her eyes spilled tears like they'd been storing them *forever*, her mascara ran, and her whitening strips filled with spit. "I'm sorry, I need a second." She pushed me out of the bathroom.

I knew it in my heart, but now it was time to see it with my own eyes. I tiptoed down the hall and opened the first door. The walls were covered with posters of majestic gymnasts flying through the air. The bed was unmade; horrible clothes were everywhere; on the floor were stacks of newspapers, scissors, food coupons. I quickly opened the next room, her mother's room, as still as death. Nothing out of place. Curtains drawn, mirrored closets closed, slippers by the untouched bed, and on the plump pillow, her medals. When I touched them, a film of dust came away on my fingers. The door squeaked. Marta was standing there. The jig was up.

Man, Life Can Suck Sometimes

With her face all streaked with mascara, her lipstick smeared, her hair a mess again, Marta stood in the doorway. If I hadn't known her, I'd have been terrified for my life. No joke. "Where's your mom, Marta?" I asked pointedly.

Marta looked around the room like it was a magical place, a secret place. "She died."

TRUE FACT: Thinking it and hearing it are two totally different things.

When she said those words, I couldn't believe it, I just couldn't. "What?" Died? As in death? I couldn't handle death. No, no, no! I sat on the edge of her dead mother's bed and had no idea what to say. All I could think of was how horrible it must be to *not* have a mother. "How the hell could that happen?" I looked at the pictures. "She's so young, healthy. An Olympic athlete, for God's sakes."

"She had a heart attack," Marta said, "in her sleep." Marta looked at the pillow where the medals were, next to my behind. "Right there."

"Yikes." I so didn't want to act like I was getting the creeps, but I was.

Marta didn't seem to notice though, luckily. "It turned out she had a leaky ventricle she never knew about."

"But when she died, how'd you manage grown-up stuff?"

"My aunt came over. She tried to take care of things, but she doesn't speak English that well." She looked around the room. "It's strange, but it's easier than you think, the details of being a grown-up. Buying food, tossing out the trash, even paying the bills was pretty easy."

I was impressed. I couldn't count the number of times I'd dreamed of just going off and being a grown-up with a trust fund.

Marta must have seen it in my eyes, because she shoved me and said, "Don't even think about it. It sucks something awful. No one cares about you; no one notices when you need a bra or when you get an A. No one screams at you when you don't pick up your room, or brush your hair, and then you just stop caring. I stopped caring about everything except gymnastics."

"But how have you been living all this time?"

"My mom was a big saver, you know, on account of her being from Romania and my dad not being around. She had life insurance, so whenever the bills come in the mail, I just pay them online. I'm good at math; I go to the market. No one ever stops me." She showed me a picture of the three of them together by the sea. "My aunt had to go back to Romania last week to fix her papers and was only going to be gone a few days, but then something happened with her visa . . . she's"— Marta took a deep breath—"she's stuck in Romania."

"Stuck? As in she-can't-come-back-and-fix-your-permit stuck?"

She got up and straightened the bed, making sure the comforter was perfectly in place. She wanted to leave. "Do you think you can get Trixie to lay off me for one more week? My aunt will be back. I'll have her get the permit, it'll all be legal, I swear, just a week, that's all I need."

"Are you kidding me? Trixie? She's probably already got her parents on it as we speak." I took a deep breath and walked out of her mom's room and down the hall. I checked my watch. Seven o'clock. Crap, I had to call home. "Can I use your phone?"

"Sure."

Pen answered with "Uh, you know it's a school night, right?" And "You think hanging out in Trixie's pool all night is gonna get you anywhere—"

"I'm at Marta's, all right?" I said. "Mom and Dad know too, so don't even try—"

192

"At Marta's?"

I held out the phone. "Marta, say something in Romanian, will ya?" Marta went into a handstand and rattled off something in Romanian while upside down. "See?"

Pen yelped. "Did you spend the forty bucks?" She was getting all excited. "Did you get her something sparkly—they love sparkles, those people—"

"No, Pen, I've been a little too tied up to shop." Jeez, where was Jai when I needed him? "Just tell Mom and Dad I'll be home by eight." I looked over at Marta. "And if I'm late, cover for me."

"You got it." She said it like she actually liked me instead of tolerated me. FYI, you can tell the difference. "And PS I want the forty bucks back."

"Yeah, yeah, yeah." I hung up and went over to where Marta's face was now a deep reddish purple. "Marta, give the handstand a rest? I need a computer, preferably one from this century."

She jumped down. "Coming right up."

A museum piece, that's what she brought out. She could barely lift the old geezer, it was so old and heavy. *Bam!* She dropped it with a clang on the coffee table.

If Jai could see this, he'd die. "You've got to be kidding." I got up and looked for the plug.

Marta watched. "What are you gonna do?"

"Your thing is gymnastics; my thing is making these things

sing." I stretched out my fingers, cracked the old knuckles, and logged on to the Los Angeles Unified School District's convoluted website. Wow, the website was a behemoth of a system, old and hard to navigate. Junk. Crap. They should just hire me to fix it.

First I had to get into the personnel section. I attempted to log in by using their real user names, which are usually some super simple combination of their first and last names, like pwest for Pam West. Next I tried to figure out passwords based on combining usernames, possible birthdates, and cell numbers, all of which were easy to find on the web if you knew someone's name. Once I had the password, then I'd be able to access the permits section and update Marta's expired permit.

"What was your mom's name?"

She was in the middle of splits, of course. "Olga Cochenko. She was so beautiful, she could fly." Marta got tears in her eyes. "But my dad, Boris Urloff, not so beautiful. He pushed her so hard, she snapped all the ligaments in her knee." She stopped and got up.

I don't know how long it took me to get that old computer buzzin'. All I can say is when I looked up, it was pitch-black outside, my shirt was covered in sweat, my fingers ached, but when that email confirmation popped up stating that Marta Urloff's permit for Happy Canyon was renewed for one full school year, I knew I was destined for greatness.

"You did it?" she said, shocked.

"Yep." I showed her the confirmation. "You're permitted for another year at Happy Canyon. And no one can take it away."

She began to cry.

I got a Kleenex and handed it to her. "Now listen, Marta, listen carefully. They're after you, you know that, right?"

"Yeah." She blew.

"If you drop the idea of the team, they'll leave you alone."

She shook her head. "Never."

"Okay, then be prepared. That permit will buy you time, and so will whatever lies I tell them. But get your aunt back here as soon as you can. You could lose everything." I left the makeup, brush, and teeth whiteners on the table and reminded her again not to forget the teeth. Shiny white teeth were key. I walked to the door. "How often do the buses come?"

"Every fifteen minutes."

"I've got to get out of here." And then I remembered one last thing, a thing of utmost importance. "Marta, please use *a lot* of deodorant tomorrow, and please, please check your teeth before you go out onstage. We don't need a piece of tuna in the teeth, if you know what I mean."

"Will you be there," she asked timidly, "tomorrow?"

"Wouldn't miss it for the world." I did a little cheer and threw up a high five. "You're going all the way, Marta Urloff. All the way."

I walked down the broken walkway, where dandelions grew

tall and strong without fear of ever getting picked. But I picked one. I closed my eyes, made a wish, and blew as hard as I could. So many seeds flew through the air, but all I needed was just one of them to come true. Just one.

The Day of Reckoning

"Happy Friday morning to you!" Mr. L started out as he always did, with a clueless smile and a crazy tie. "Today is a big day for—" He scanned the class for Trixie and Marta. "Where are they? They can't both be gone!" He jotted down the names of the tardy. "Probably sleeping in. Well, anyway, a big day in sports and also a big day for our Emperor Caesar, right?" The class groaned. "Open your Ancient Roman history books to—"

Trix and Babs ran in, out of breath. "So sorry! So sorry we're late." Trix looked straight at me, mad as you-know-what. *Where have you been?* she mouthed. *Huh?*

"Books, please!" Mr. L shouted. And I was grateful. For one hour we studied pointless Rome, but all I did was watch the door. Marta, where was Marta? I didn't even care that

Bobby was flirting with me by trying to knock over my backpack. Where. Was. Marta? When the bell rang at ten o'clock for nutrition, I got up to go look for her, but Trix—and her follower, Babs—blocked me from leaving.

Trixie came over to my desk, arms folded, bearing down on me. "I didn't sleep, you know. Not good for competition day."

Babs threw her hands in the air. "Seriously, Charlie, where have you been?"

"I'm sorry, I got home super late." I pulled out my lunch. "Her mom works long hours—it's crazy."

Babs's mouth dropped open. "Her mom? You actually saw her?"

"Yeah, yeah." I acted as casual as I could. "Like at eight or something. Boy, does she work late." I got up and tried to leave, but still they wouldn't move. Did I mention I can't maintain eye contact when I lie? "Can I go now?"

"No, you cannot go." Trixie glared.

"What? Why?" I rolled my eyes. "Look, I did what you asked. I went, I waited, I saw her mom, who drives one of those corn cars." I laughed. "She's really into saving the environment," I added for detail. "Can we just move on and have some fun already?"

Trixie was bone still, her hands flat on my desk. "*I don't believe you!*"

I could see her sequined leotard under her sweater. "You gotta let this go. We did all we could." I looked into her now-raging eyes.

"Did you?" She looked unconvinced. "Really, Charlie?"

"Yes." I was exhausted. "Come on, Trix, let's think about fun stuff, like the Halloween party. What are you gonna be, huh?"

"You don't think I know?"

Here it comes. My past catching up with me.

"I've known all along, Charlie." She looked evil. "I've just been waiting for that perfect moment to let it out."

I could feel my heart racing. My face burned with shame. "So what's stopping you?"

"I've been waiting to see whose side you're really on." Trixie looked into my eyes like she was trying to suck information from my brain.

"Yours." I gulped.

Her eyes narrowed. Our noses were nearly touching. "I'm not sure I believe you."

TRUE FACT: Playing both sides makes you seriously hungry.

"Are you kidding me? After all I've done for you?" I yelled, indignant. "I'm not friends with Marta. I feel sorry for her, that's all."

"So sorry you want her to win?"

"No," I said. "I want you to win."

"Good," she said calmly. "Then from now on, stay out of it, hear me?"

My stomach tightened.

"Hear me?" she repeated. "Because whenever you get in it, for some strange reason, things seem to work in Marta's favor, *not* mine."

"I won't do anything else," I promised.

"If you do anything to stop me from winning, you will pay, you hear me?"

"I do," I said, realizing that I was, in fact, a big, fat coward. They'd started to walk away when off in the distance, near the lower parking lot, there was a horrible noise. An entire metal bookcase had fallen to the ground. The art teacher scrambled to pick up the drawings before the wind carried them away. Trixie stood watching her pick up all the pieces. Babs suddenly ran over and joined her at the top of the steps.

"Look!" Babs pointed at something in the distance. She whispered in Trixie's ear. I could see Trixie's evil smile from a mile away.

I ran over to where they stood, to see what they were looking at, but Trixie quickly put her arm around my neck and turned me around. The bell rang. She whispered, "Plan B, Charlie, Plan B. Now go away." And they ran off down the stairs to the parking lot in the opposite direction of class.

Lunch rolled around, and Marta still wasn't at school. Trixie's mood went from raving lunatic to cloud nine. Everywhere she went, people asked where Marta was, and I could hear her say with absolute certainty, "Yeah, maybe Marta realized she's no team player," as though it was a done deal that she wasn't coming. Or "I heard her permit expired, poor thing." And "Yeah, she's really good, it's true, and I wish her the best, but—"

Her change in mood scared the crap out of me. Could Trixie be so demented that she'd actually do something to stop Marta from competing? I knew Marta, and I knew nothing would keep her from this day. At lunch, when no one was looking, I ran home. Outside, there were bulldozers, bricklayers, electricians, carpenters. Dad saw me running through and stopped me. "Uh, what are you doing here?"

"Forgot my homework." I pointed to my room, huffing and puffing. "Is Mom in there?"

"She's working on the rock walls." He nodded. "Around back." Then he gave me one of those looks like he could see through me. "You sure nothing's the matter?"

"Just forgot the homework, trying to be all I can be, you know the slogan." I jumped up and kissed him.

"I always knew you had it in you." He hugged me back. "I'm so proud of you, Charlie." And then he got that look parents get when they know you're *not* telling them something, but they'll give you a pass anyway. "See you tonight."

"See ya!" I ran into the house and grabbed the phone. The refrigerator door closed, *bam!* And guess who was there? Mom. And she didn't look all that happy to see me. "And what are you doing home, young lady?" She got closer. "You know, just because you live near school doesn't mean you can take off whenever you feel like it."

"Forgot my homework," I said as fast as I could.

She folded her arms and took a step closer. "Lie." See, even if she were blindfolded, Mom could tell when I lied.

I took a step back. "Okay, fine." I twirled around. "Marta didn't turn up today, and I'm really worried—just wanted to call her, which"—I took a deep breath—"I could have done at school from my very own cell phone, if you'd buy me one."

"She's not at school?" Her super thin eyebrows got all worried. "Isn't today the big day?"

"Yeah." I nodded, scared that something really had happened to Marta.

Mom got that creepy look like Dad's, that proud look, which made my skin kinda crawl. "That girl needs to win today. Give her a call. Maybe she overslept."

I dialed. It rang forever and then clicked to a woman's voice. Her mom's voice, I think, was on the answering machine. Man, did that make me feel horrible. I don't know how she kept it. Then I thought, You know, maybe it makes her feel like her mom is still here.

I heard the beep, and I went off:

"Where the heck are you? It's today, Marta, you have to be in school ASAP!" I hung up. Looked at Mom. "Not there."

Mom took out her cell phone from her pocket. "Do you have her mom's cell-phone number?"

I was hoping she wouldn't ask me that.

"Charlie?" she pressed me.

I didn't know what to do. I was scared and in over my head, but God help me, I was no nark.

Mom put down her phone. "Baby, what aren't you telling me?" That's when Dad came walking in. "Ladies, it's looking good out there." He poured himself a tall glass of sun-kissed tea and saw that something was bothering me. "What's up?"

"Marta's not at school." Mom tapped a pencil on the counter like she was trying to piece it together.

He shrugged it off. "Maybe she's sick."

"No, Dad, she's not answering the phone. She'd never, ever miss this. You don't understand. She'd cut her arm off if she had to." I dropped my head, so they couldn't see the worry. *Oh, Marta, how can I keep your secret if you don't show up?*

"Oh, she'll show; she probably just slept in." Dad put his arm around Mom and kissed her cheek. "Or she's sick, and her mom's getting her medicine."

Mom looked at Dad. "Yeah, you're right, hon." She kissed him back. "I have a tendency to always jump to conclusions!"

No, Mom, you're right on the money! I felt like screaming. *There is no mom to take care of her; there is no sick for Marta; there are gymnastics, and that is all.*

"Go back to school, Charlie." Mom walked me to the door; she kissed me. "Marta's tough. She'll be there, unless something really serious has gotten in the way."

That's what I was afraid of. It was so unfair. I felt like crying. "She deserves it, you know? More than anyone. When she's up there, on those bars, or flying through the air, she's the most beautiful thing you've ever seen."

Mom hugged me tight. "So are you." She swatted me on the butt, pushing Dad out the door too. "Now get out of here, you two."

When we stepped out, I noticed just how crazy it was outside. There were so many tractors and backhoes, giant hoses spraying water on the digging sites, and electricians—and then I noticed he'd put a giant pot over the trapdoor to the tunnels. I whispered into his ear, "You didn't tell them yet?"

Dad looked over at Martin and all the suits with their clipboards. "Not yet."

In my opinion he was totally right not to trust them. Suits in the canyons spelled trouble.

He whispered into my ear, "My gut tells me they'll do something pretty tacky with those tunnels that I'm not too excited about."

I jumped up and kissed him. "You're a good man, Dad."

I ran back to school just in time to sit with Trix and Babs for a second before the bell rang. "Hey!" I slid onto the bench to try to get a peek at their lunches. Man, was I hungry. Of course, with all this drama, I hadn't eaten a single bite of my mozzarella-and-tomato sandwich. I took a look at Babs's lunch first, which was always hit-or-miss. Sometimes she had egg salad on whole wheat, and other times pizza. But Trix—Trix packed her lunches herself, so it was all candy, and if she felt like it, a little gourmet cheese.

But evidently Trix was not in a sharing mood, 'cause when she saw I was hungry, she scooped up all her stuff to her chest like a mean hoarder. "You always seem to be running away."

"Um, I forgot my homework at home." I chewed a nail. "Had to run all the way back. Why?"

Trix reached across and grabbed my hand, hard. Really hard. "Roxy wants to talk."

But before I had time to react, Bobby walked past. "Yo, yo, yo, Charlie!" Bobby's friends, Sam and Wyatt, walked past too. "Hey, Trix, who's gonna win?"

Trixie dropped my hand and smiled like a psycho who can't see or hear anything else besides what's in her own head. She said with a smile, "It's mine, mine, all mine." She was seriously losing it, which was crazy. If I had her pool, her house, Esmerelda, I'd never ask for a single thing again for as long as I lived.

The bell rang; it was already twelve thirty. We all got up and went back to class. Two more hours until showtime, and all I could think about was where the heck was that Marta?

The Moment You're Never Going to Believe

When that final bell rang at two forty-five, the entire school poured into the upper yard and then into the room where Marta and Trixie were set to square off. But there was no Marta. A rumor was going around that she was just coming in for the competition, but I still had a bad feeling that something had gone wrong.

I opened the door and *man!* Talk about the need to reapply! It stank like a butcher shop on a hot day. Every seat was taken, of course; everyone was there for one reason: Marta's humiliation. Trix had spread the word. They were out for blood. That's what they did to me too—the whole school came to watch me get kicked out.

TRUE FACT: Humans love watching other humans get humiliated.

It all gave me a horrible bout of post-traumatic stress disorder, with a touch of nausea. I nearly sprained my ankle just trying to run over all those legs I saw. Bobby saw me coming. His mouth was full of Cheetos. Man, I loved Cheetos. "Marta's gonna lose. You know that, right?"

But I didn't care. "Have you seen her? Please tell me she came late—"

Bobby shook his head and stuck his orange fingers in his orange mouth. "Nope, haven't smelled her all day."

"And that's a good thing," his buddy Sam said, "because, no matter what she does, it ain't gonna be pretty."

I looked at them, wondering how everyone just kept going along with the way things were when the way things were *sucked*. "And you think that's okay?"

Bobby shrugged. "It's just the way it is. Yo, Sam, you comin'? This is gonna be hys-ter-i-cal." And they disappeared, laughing their heads off, into the overcrowded sweat hall.

I screamed after them, "Go, you dumb lambs!" The door closed, I watched from outside through the little square glass. I was so focused on searching for Marta, on willing her to arrive, that I didn't even notice when Trixie suddenly popped up at my side.

"That Roxy!" She shook her head slowly. "She is sooooo mad at you still, my goodness!" And then she rolled those baby blues like I'd seen her do way too many times. "I tried to tell her that you'd changed, that you were, well, normal, but

Roxy would not have it."

"Thanks," I said, but I wanted to slap her.

She looked at me with suspicion. "What are you doing out here, Charlie?"

"Watching you win, of course!" I threw my hands in the air like a lame cheerleader. "Yeah!"

"Really?" She folded her arms. "'Cause to me it looks like you're waiting for Farta, which I can't imagine, because if you were a real friend, you wouldn't even be thinking of her. You'd be thinking of me."

"Which I am." I pointed to the door. "By making absolutely sure that Marta doesn't turn up, I *am* thinking of you, don't you see?"

"You know what?" Her face got all scrunched up like she was about to attack, but then the door flew open and Lillian grabbed Trixie's hand.

She was bouncing up and down. "Marta's missed her slot! You're up now," Lillian said, beaming, "so don't blow it."

I watched from outside as Trixie hopped out of her sparkly white-and-silver tracksuit. I spotted Felix in the crowd, but not Pen. I wondered where she was, why she wasn't at the school's biggest day of the year. Trixie stood on the mat, raised her hands high in the air, and then, like a bullet, took off running. It was the same routine she'd been practicing every day; and she'd gotten it down to a science, no mistakes, but she kinda looked like a possessed robot. Even I knew that no matter how hard she wanted it, she didn't have what it took to be great. The dumb crowd roared anyway. Did they even know the difference? Did they care? Nah.

Lillian came out, picked up the microphone, and said, "Ladies and gentlemen, a nearly perfect routine. She already looks like part of the team. And so cute too, don't you think?"

The crowd chanted, "Trixie! Trixie!" And Trixie soaked it up like a dry sponge.

I wanted to cry. The injustice just pissed me off so much, you have no idea. Dang it, Marta! Where the heck were you?! What could have kept you from this? I ran to the parking lot, looking down the street toward the lower yard. Nowhere. I ran back just in time to see Lillian on the microphone again (boy, did she love that microphone). I ran inside the gym.

"Well, the clocks are ticking. We've got about fifteen more minutes"—she batted her silver lashes, letting the room fill with whistles and cheers—"before we can announce our winner." She glanced at Trixie. They shared a smile.

When Trixie saw me, she came running over. "Did you see, did you see me?"

"You were great," I said, and then I realized that Babs was gone. In fact, Babs had been gone for a while. "Where's Babs?"

Trixie hugged me with her little, twisted bird arms and put her lips up against my ear. "We took care of it."

I froze. "What do you mean?"

"It's done," she said. "As the French say, a fait accompli."

"Where is she, Trixie?" I asked with a deadly calm.

She shrugged, looking up at the classrooms that lined the upper yard. "It's so easy to get lost here, in this place"—she smiled—"when you're not from here."

I took off running.

"Where are you going?" She laughed at me, but I did not care. I was at a serious disadvantage; I did not know this place at all. I ran upstairs to the third floor, where there were only two classrooms open. I'd heard Mr. Lawson say they locked this floor half the time—if I were hiding something, I'd hide it here. The halls were dark, and super creepy without kids. "Marta!" I screamed into one room, then another. In the bathroom, the hall closet, the cleaning closet:

"Marta!

"Marta!

"Marta!"

I hopped the stairs to one level down and crossed the bridge into the high school area of the campus, another great place to stash someone. I hit the top floor and ran, screaming "Marta!" up and down the empty hallways. I yanked doors open, calling her name each time. I was running out of breath and out of time. Soon Trixie would just ease in and take her spot.

I dropped down a floor and checked each and every room,

listening for strange noises. "Marta!" I yelled, and then stopped to listen closely. "Where are you?!" I grabbed my hair, wishing I could yank it all off, about ready to give up, when a door opened, and I saw Pen. My Pen. "Pen!"

She came over quickly. "What are you doing here?"

"Looking for Marta." I tried to catch my breath. "I think they did something with her, put her somewhere—"

Pen looked horrified. "You really think Trixie would do that?"

"The stakes are high," I said. "Too high. We're talking real-world stuff."

Pen looked around, paced in a tight circle. I could tell that her brain was working, and when her brain was working, she almost always got the right answer.

"Well, there's a giant art room that only the teachers know about, and me, because I'm spearheading an art program for kids with anger problems. You should try it—"

"Stop, all right!" I shook my head. "There's no way they're gonna stash her in the—"

"You're not listening to me." Pen shook my shoulders. "In the *always* empty unused parking lot?"

"What?" And then it hit me. The commotion earlier, and the look on Trixie's face. Could Babs have been pointing at Marta coming up the road from the bus stop? Did they get her to go into the art room somehow and then just lock the door on her?

Pen nodded as though reading my mind. "Soundproof, far away, and you can lock it."

What a perfect place to stash a screamer. I hugged her. "You're brilliant!"

I was about to take off when Pen ran back inside and opened her teacher's desk. "We'll need these."

A huge ring of stolen keys, yes! "Keys! Fantastic!" We ran down the stairs and into the high school art room. Pen banged on the heavy metal door. "Marta!" I screamed. "You in here?"

Mumbling.

"Marta?" More mumbling. I looked at Pen. "She's here! She's in here!"

Pen put a key in and opened the door, and there she was, Marta, slumped against the wall, makeup streaked, snot all over the place, super ugly tracksuit covered in—on second thought, I didn't want to know. "Oh my God, Marta, are you okay?"

Marta glared at me, wild-eyed, and asked about the only thing she really ever cared about. "Is there still time?"

"Yeah, yeah." I grabbed a paper towel and put water on it. Marta strained to get out like a boxer strains to get across the ring to kick some serious butt, and I couldn't wait to see her kick. "Wash your face," I said calmly. "You have to look beautiful, remember." I finger-combed her hair, slapped her cheeks for color. Slapped them again just for the fun of it. Pen handed me some lip gloss and mascara that she kept in her purse, and voilà! Marta didn't even look like a hostage anymore.

"You're going to win, Marta," Pen said, all maturelike, "because it is right that you win."

I pushed open the door. "Make your mama proud!"

The Moment of Truth

I peeked through the glass and saw Marta walking onto the center mat, in the new red-and-white leotard she'd bought before her mom died—all elastic intact, not a single nipple showing! Hallelujah! Even from outside, I could tell that everyone's mouth was *wide open*. You *could* have heard a pin drop. *No joke.* Even with the mascara streaked, the red and puffy eyes, Marta walked in like she was a new person, and the whole world watched. Confident. Graceful. Beautiful. And one heck of a bob, courtesy of yours truly.

Pen came up beside me. "Wow."

"Just look at her, will ya!" I squealed.

TRUE FACT: I was proud. Proud of her and proud of me.

"Like Cinderella." Pen couldn't stop smiling. She pulled open the door, and we slid in behind the standing crowds.

Marta stood before the judges' table a totally different person. I heard her say sweetly, which you may recall was so unlike her, "I'm sorry I'm late. May I please start?"

When Lillian laid eyes on her, she could hardly keep her mouth closed, she was that shocked. "Oh my God, you're so, so pretty—"

Pen was watching Trixie. "She really put her in there?"

You could see it from where we stood. Daggers were shooting out of those ice-blue eyes straight at yours truly. What she had planned for me I could only guess. "Yep."

The teammates, aka mean girls, had gathered into a group, with Coach in the middle. They were talking, then arguing, until Coach slammed down his palm. There was a shocked silence. Coach won that round. He emerged from the group looking like a Russian bear, pointing at her. "Now, Marta."

The energy in the room was insane; the tension, the excitement, the disbelief. And yet, standing here, I felt like I already knew the ending. Marta would not fail.

"Watch this," I mumbled to my sister as Marta stretched her long arms across her chest. "Her mother was an Olympic gymnast from Romania; she trained with the greats."

My heart beat hard as I watched Marta walk to the end of the mat and point her arms up. And then, like a bolt, she ran faster, stronger, better than anyone had ever seen before. She looked like an engine, her body transformed into something so sharp, so perfect, so fast, it was like a whirling blade as she floored it to the springboard. When she bounced, she flew so high, all necks snapped backward so as not to miss an instant. In seconds she completed a series of flips and jackknives that were so fast, they blurred. Next it was the uneven bars, Trixie's area of expertise, and Marta was swinging from them, slapping against them, flipping between them like she lived on them. The room held its breath as she readied her dismount; you could feel the expectation as she revved up for it, built to it, and then dismounted into a backflip that was so gravity defying, that when she landed on both feet, and her arms shot up, the silence was deafening.

"What!" Pen stopped blinking. "Is that even physically possible?"

"I know, it's crazy," I said. "And she can do it all, floor, rings, uneven, vault, all of it."

And then, like a slow wave along the packed bleachers, everyone got up. The room exploded. Coach jumped out of his seat and saluted her. Lillian got up. Everyone clapped so hard, their hands must have bled. But they didn't stop clapping.

The crowd had all but forgotten that, just that morning, Marta had been nothing more than despicable Marta the Farta. They went wild, chanting, "Marta! Marta!"

The coach marched over to her, his eyes red and swollen with tears, his giant potato of a nose leaking. "You will take us to the Nationals, Marta Urloff, and you will go all the way to the Olympics. Mark my words!" My ears were picking up bits and pieces of conversation like:

"Man, Farta's not that bad."

"Dude, she's kinda hot."

"I know, right!"

Marta turned and scanned the crowd. I knew she was looking for me, and I was proud. I threw up my hand, and she picked me out, hidden behind a row of people. She looked right at me and nodded her head so slightly, you'd never know. But I knew.

Pen hit me on the shoulder. "You did good, kid."

I was just about to say thanks, to tell her how good it felt, when I saw Trixie walking calmly through the cheering crowd, her head bowed, with one single tear of black mascara dribbling down her silver cheek. Babette was right behind her, repeating, "It's gonna be okay, Trix, you'll make it next year." Trix pushed through the door.

Pen shook her head. "There's gonna be hell to pay."

I knew exactly what she meant, but I could not run from it. I went outside to find Trixie waiting for me. She had an eerie, calm look to her like that super creepy girl in that *Orphan* movie who looked like a ninety-nine-year-old lady who loved killing people. "It was you, wasn't it?"

Inside, people were still cheering, yelling, all in shock over Marta's total change.

Trixie looked up. "It was you, you did that hair, that face, those teeth, it was you, all you."

I nodded. "Yeah, it was me."

She nodded. "She looks beautiful."

Say what? I stared. Where was the rant? Where was the anger, hatred, retribution?

Bobby and his small gang of followers came bouncing over, full of adrenaline. He leaned into me. "Marta was awesome; she even looked not half bad. You saw it all along too. Way to go, Charlie."

"Yep," Trixie said, looking at Bobby, "did she ever."

Babs watched Bobby, shaking her head. "But didn't you see Trixie? She was amazing; she totally deserved it."

"Yeah, right!" Bobby laughed and walked off.

"Jerk!" Babs screamed after him.

But Trixie put up her hand. "Stop, stop, Babs. She deserves it, all right."

TRUE FACT: I knew Trixie would come up with something truly evil to get back at me, but the game was in motion, and I could not stop playing.

I rubbed her shoulder. "You're taking this incredibly well."

"I thought I was super clear with you earlier." She pulled her shoulder away, picked up her gym bag, and narrowed her eyes.

"You were," I said.

She nodded. "So you know what's going to happen to you?"

"Oh, there are lots of possibilities," I said, and was just about to tell her it had been so worth it when people began pouring out of the gym. Lillian and her teammates came first; then Coach and Marta followed behind. Coach was going on and on, his accent so thick it was hard to understand a single word, when suddenly he grabbed his heart like he was having a heart attack.

"That's it!" His sausage finger was in Marta's face, his shiny Windbreaker heaving with his enormous stomach. "It's been bothering me all week, I couldn't make sense of it before, but now I know who it is you remind me of." He took a breath as though sad. "Olga Cochenko."

Trixie's whole head spun around. "Who? What?"

Oh no! Oh no! I tried to get her attention, but she was gone before I could stop her. "Trix, wait up!" I called after her, but she'd joined the ever-growing circle listening to Coach.

"She was the greatest of her time!" he yelled out like he was announcing it to the world. "She was powerful, beautiful, and angry"—and then he pointed—"like you, Marta."

I noticed Marta's eyes getting all misty. Trixie must have noticed it too.

"When I saw you the first time, it was like a ghost walked across my heart. I got this sensation that I knew you, your moves, your spirit, your drive. You're identical, do you know that?" He leaned into her like a father leans into his daughter.

"Have you been told that before?"

Erica looked over at Lillian. "Didn't she get, like, two silvers and a bronze?"

"She was incredible. Her floor routine was the best since—" Lillian closed her eyes.

Without thinking, Marta finished her sentence. "Since Comăneci."

"Uh, excuse me." Trixie dropped her bag; her voice rose above all the chatter. "But didn't Olga Cochenko *die* last year?"

"Uh, I don't watch TV." Marta looked like she was about to jump right out of her candy-apple-red leotard. "My mom is waiting for me. I gotta go."

Trixie walked right up to her face, so they were chin to chin. Before my eyes, I saw her confidence returning with force. "Your mom isn't really waiting for you, is she, Marta?"

And Marta's confidence disappeared with equal force. Her face grew twisted; she panicked. "I gotta go."

"Go, go." Trixie nodded like a patronizing nurse. "I'm sure she'll be so happy for you." And then she added, just to show us that she would never let this go. "She'll be at all the meets too, right?"

"Yeah." Marta couldn't get out of there fast enough. "Thanks, Coach, team, see you on Monday."

I was just about to ask her to come over to my house when Pickler came running up out of nowhere. We all thought it was to congratulate Marta, but we were wrong.

TRUE FACT: Principals *love* it when someone tattles *directly* to them. Otherwise they feel like they just don't matter.

"Trixie Chalice," he announced into the courtyard, and everybody turned. "Your parents are waiting for you in my office."

"Why, sir?" She looked at him like he was nuts. "I didn't do anything."

With his hands on his small hips, he narrowed his little eyes and said, "I don't call locking your classmate in the art room so that you can win nothing. To my office *now!*" He pointed to his door, but she wasn't budging.

I saw Pen in the background. Oh God, Pen, what did you do?

Lillian and Erica stepped away from Trixie like she was suddenly carrying some gross disease.

"What?" Trixie stared them down. "What are you whispering about, huh? Huh?"

Babs threw up her hand. "It was me, it was me!"

But Pickler wasn't biting. "Now, Ms. Chalice."

Pickler winked at Marta. "You were stupendous. Good job, ladies. Coach, we're going to the Nationals, am I right?" He pulled Trixie's sleeve. "Young lady, my office, now."

I gulped. Marta was speechless. The girls watched Trixie being led away and Babs following, pleading, "But really it was me, it was me, take me!" she cried, and followed them all into the office.

"Poor girl," I said.

"She deserves it," Pen shot back, about to launch into her version of the I Have a Dream speech when I cut her off.

"I was talking about Babs," I said.

Coach looked at his watch. "It's late, Marta. We'll talk next week." He nodded at his future team. "Good night."

Lillian and Erica came up to Marta. They were both so much taller than Marta that they kind of stood over her. "Is your mother Cochenko?"

I was about to step in with some fantastic lie when Marta's eyes grew steely and cold. "She was my aunt. My mother, also a gymnast, was her sister."

Lillian and Erica looked at each other and shrugged. "Why didn't you say that, then?" They threw their arms around each other and walked out of the courtyard, most probably to one of their houses, where their parents had dinner waiting for the "team." They did not invite her.

"Good one," I said as we watched them go, but Marta didn't answer. She just stood there with the saddest look on her face.

"They'll never accept me," she said. "No matter what I look like, how great a gymnast I become." She dropped her head. "Never."

I thought of my man, Houdini, and knew that there were many times in his life when he must have thought the same thing. He even married a woman whose parents hated him, but he didn't let that stop him. He let nothing stop him. Marta needed a little Houdini in her life. "Hey, want to come over to my house? We can celebrate."

She looked taken aback. "Me?"

"Yeah, you. It's a little loud, a little crazy. I have a little brother too; he's a total psycho."

"Yeah, sure," she said, like she didn't really care. But I knew she did. She grabbed her gym bag, and we walked down the darkening canyon together, breathing in the mist that came through most nights and settled over us like an old ghost.

Marta Gets All Heavy

We celebrated that night. The way Mom and Dad acted, it was like one of their own had made it onto the team. While Mom threw together a Duncan Hines devil's food cake and a tray of lasagna, Marta walked around the estate, examining the rock walls, fountains, springs, and statues like an explorer, both amazed and strangely sad. I wanted to ask her why, but I knew why. She kicked butt in the gym, but out of it, she was scared. And who could blame her? She had no one.

"As soon as your aunt is back, you'll be fine," I said, "and in the meantime, you can stay here."

She looked confused. "Why are you so nice to me?"

I had no idea how to answer that. "Um, well, I—" She stared at me like she really wanted the answer.

And then, thank God, Mom opened the door and called,

"Girls!" Boy, was I glad for the interruption. I wasn't in the mood for a confession. So I ran in, and Marta came after me. The lights were out, but when we came in, Dad, Mom, Felix, and Pen all started screaming and switching the lights on and off.

"Congratulations!" they yelled. On the table was Mom's yellow Provence tablecloth that she *loved*, flowers from the garden, a huge bowl of salad (*yuck*), lasagna, and the cake. Mom came over and gave Marta a kiss. And you know what? Marta actually let herself be kissed. "I only wish your mom didn't have to work," said Mom.

Marta had tears in her eyes looking at all of us. "Why?" she asked again.

"Why what?" Dad looked at her like he had no idea what she was talking about 'cause he didn't. Marta was not normal, if you get my drift.

"Why are you all so nice to me? I've never been nice; I am not nice as a person." Marta looked at her hands. She spread them out, stared at the calluses. "I've always been tough. People don't like me."

"That's how Charlie was," Felix said, picking up his plate, "and she's nice now. People change."

Mom got up and started serving everyone. "Your life will only get better from now on. You're on the team. Those girls will come to see you as the incredibly valuable person you are."

Pen shook her head. "Who knows what Trixie's gonna do

after Pickler's through with her?" And then she brightened. "But at least you're free and clear, Marta. She can never hurt you again. Cheers to that!"

Ha! If she only knew the half of it, she'd bury her head in the sand like one of those blindworms and never come out. I had so many balls in the air, I felt like a juggler. To recap:

1. Trixie was a complete psycho.
2. The permit was a total fake.
3. Marta was an orphan living in Reseda illegally.
4. Roxy's last promise to me was to hunt me down and tell everyone how truly desperate I was.

TRUE FACT: Grudges are seriously unattractive.

But back to Pen, who had that satisfied look all over her face like she'd just fed the last hungry child. "Enough of this negativity; let's celebrate."

That night Marta promised me that she'd have her next-door neighbor come and stay if I promised to look into her aunt's paperwork. I could not promise—the US immigration department was a tough nut to crack, and my Romanian was a little rusty—but I planned on calling Jai as soon as she left to see what we could do. Jai was a master at booking first-class flights and flying all over the world without paying a single cent.

"Lock your doors," I yelled out as she was leaving. "Don't open them for anyone."

She turned, still wearing her pink princess velour sweat-pants over her leotard. Mom and Dad came to the window and watched her go. Dad mumbled, "That girl just might go all the way."

Mom shook her head. "So independent, too."

"European kids are so much more self-sufficient," Dad said, and elbowed me.

"You're right about that." I grinned, because sometimes some things were better not said. She got on the little bus, put her hand on the window, and disappeared up Laurel Canyon Boulevard.

Travel Plans

I spent most of Saturday holed up in my room with Jai on the other side of the screen as we entered the false information of Greta Cochenko, making her a Romanian citizen with an H-1B visa allowing her to live in the United States temporarily. This required a string of heavily encrypted code that made us both want to pull our hair out, but it was the best we could do. Any kind of sudden change to a permanent resident visa would have raised too many red flags.

"This is what it must have felt like for all those spies," Jai said, stretching. He had a single lightbulb over his laptop. I could hear his family snoring. The bunch of ingrates; they should have been massaging his shoulders. "Getting into President Putin's personal Mac was easier than this, Charlie."

We were done. "Jai, my friend"—I stood, stretched, cracked

my back—"I owe you." I couldn't wait to tell Marta to call her aunt and tell her to get her butt to the airport. Her H-1B visa was in the system. Kids, do not try this one at home.

The moment I hung up, I called Marta. But when she picked up, she sounded crazed. "Whoa, calm down, calm down, what's wrong?" I said.

"They're outside my house, Charlie. They're sitting across the street in Trixie's housekeeper's car." She swallowed like someone who hasn't had anything to drink for a long time. "They're watching me."

"Since when?"

"Since I got back from your house last night." She was hyperventilating.

"Oh crap," I said. I told her about the papers. "Call your aunt now. She's booked on a British Airways flight out of Bucharest International on Monday nine forty a.m. to London, and then it's on to LA, business class—we decided first class might draw attention. She's landing at eleven forty-five p.m. Monday night."

"I'm not gonna last that long. They're going to call Social Services. I swear, they know."

"Have you left the house?"

"No," she said. "I'm too scared."

"You have to leave!" I said. "You have to act normal, go next door, visit your neighbor, walk around, play outside, sit on the stoop. Marta, don't just hide behind the curtain in there like you're a crazy bomber."

"I feel sick." She whimpered. Very unlike her, I might add.

"Marta." I got very quiet. "Call your aunt now. Have her call British Airways or log onto their website. She will see her booking. Tell her to pack a bag and get to the airport first thing Monday morning. When she lands on Monday night, and those little passport checkers look her up, she should have a beautiful visa by her name and be welcomed home with loving arms."

"I don't know, I don't know, I don't know—" she cried.

"Pull it together!" I yelled. "If all goes well, she'll be here on Monday night. Marta, relax, we did it!"

"Promise me you won't tell your parents, promise me!" She was almost hysterical. "I know what they do to people like me. They send them to horrible places, places where I'll never get to do gymnastics again."

"Yeah, yeah, yeah." Jeez when did I become the good guy? Being nice was getting seriously exhausting.

It Just Gets Worse

But when the alarm clock went off on Monday morning, I was full of dread. I knew that today was the day it would all happen, and I had to be totally ready for anything that came my way. First things first, clear the decks:

I shot an email to Dr. Scales and decided to be honest because of the whole doctor-patient privilege thing.

Dear Dr. Scales,

I'm going to have to cancel our usual session, because today's the day it's all going down. If I end up in jail, or worse, Romanian jail, I want you to know that:

1. It's pretty much all your fault.
2. My heart was in the right place.
3. I'm probably going to need a lawyer.

231

I was about to hit Send when I remembered the clause that said if a patient confesses to something against the law, it was the doctor's duty to tell. I looked at Mr. Mandela and Mr. Jobs, took a deep breath, hit Delete, then wrote:

Dear Dr. Scales,

Sadly my teacher, Mr. Lawson, has scheduled another trip to the pound today, so I will have to cancel. I'd like to reschedule for tomorrow, Tuesday, if you're free.

Who was I kidding? Of course he was free.

Doc,

Please read your email! Write me back. I'll see you tomorrow.

Charlie C. Cooper

I put on my lucky black leggings with holes, a black lace tank top, and some serious high-top Nikes. I pulled my hair into a loose loop up on top of my head and got out my sandalwood beads. The gurus use them to slow down, to count until their minds are clear again. I had a feeling the beads might come in handy.

"It's gonna be okay." Pen could see the stress all over me. She rubbed my shoulders. "What else can Trixie do to her? It's done, finished, over."

I didn't say anything. What could I say? My parents would kill me if they knew how deep into this I'd gotten myself.

"Have a great day." Mom kissed us all.

"Oh, Mom, I almost forgot," I said. "Scales sent me an email; he had to cancel today."

Her mom antennae shot up. "Really? He said nothing to me."

I nodded, not looking in her eyes. "Yeah, we're on for tomorrow afternoon though."

"Oh, okay." Mom antennae down.

When we walked out the door, it was misty and slow outside. I got that feeling again, like the end of the world was coming. I wondered if this was how the Incans felt every day.

Dad was riding one of the tractors, a huge smile on his face. I immediately felt guilty. He was so much happier here than he was building mansions for all those rich Hollywood types. What if I got into serious trouble, and he got fired? And we got kicked out? What if?

Felix pushed me from behind. "Come on, we're gonna miss the bell." As we came up to school, buses and cars edged into the lot and kids walked past, but the three of us stood on the corner, watching.

Pen took a deep breath like it was a glorious day. "Marta's going to become our national hero, just watch."

Not if she's in foster care in South Central. I pointed to Pen's braces. "You've got a strawberry in your braces, right there."

"Thanks," she said, and we all walked in.

What did I expect Trixie to do to me? I didn't have a clue. All my senses were on red alert. I was like a ninja this morning, I'm telling you, one beautiful ninja.

It all started off smoothly. The morning began with a huge round of applause for both Trixie and Marta. A standing ovation. Marta looked massively uncomfortable when Mr. L asked her to stand.

"Thanks," she said, and immediately sat back down. I could see in seconds that she'd been biting her lips and nails all weekend, had barely slept, and forget about combing her hair—the matted knots were back. Trixie, on the other hand, beamed like the real champion.

"Thank you," she said, waving. Then she held her hands to her heart. "All your support has meant the world."

I wondered what kind of punishment Pickler had handed out; whatever it was it couldn't have been bad. She was positively glowing, the evil witch.

Mr. Lawson cleared his throat. "All right, there will be plenty more time to celebrate Marta's win later. You're practicing today, am I right?"

Marta nodded. I checked Lillian's face, stone cold. Trix and Babs looked like it was the last day of school. You know that glint in the eye, that excitement that comes from knowing what's just about to happen?

"Take out your books on Rome, people." He walked around

us. "Unlike this group here, we're going to talk about backstabbing, mistrust, treachery Roman style."

How apt. I opened my book, and a note flew out and landed like a pebble on my desk. On it was written: *She's coming for you. Watch out.*

I turned to see who wrote it, but all heads were down.

After a good half hour, Mr. Lawson stopped reading from his boring book, looked up, and said, "Boy, you kids sure are tired today." He sounded amazed. "Not a peep, no flying notes, secret signs? You're really maturing."

TRUE FACT: Teachers are so clueless, it's scary.

Yep, Mr. L, you nailed it right on the head. We were maturing. Were all teachers this out of touch with their students? They were more in tune with a Roman senator's murderous rage from thousands of years ago than what was brewing before their eyes in their very own classrooms.

The next period bell rang. And when it did, people did not jump and run as they always did. They moved slowly. Bobby looked at his pack of friends; Trixie looked at Babs; Lillian at Erica. The undercurrent was so intense, it felt like I was about to get zapped by an electrical fence. I put my hands on my beads and counted.

"Come on." Marta slapped me on the back. "We've got PE."

I'd totally forgotten.

Today of all days we had the big nine-lap run—one whole horrible mile. Talk about child abuse. I went into the locker room to change. I took a super long time, because I *refuse* to change in public and had to wait for a stall to open. Here's why:

1. No one was gonna talk about my boobs (or lack of boobs) at the next party I was *not* invited to.
2. I would not be judged naked.
3. Naked people seriously grossed me out.

When I finally got a stall—Mitzi Warner, the fattest girl in school, was in there for like an hour—it was so quiet in the bathroom, I thought I was alone. But when I came out of the toilet stall, changed and ready to run, I stopped dead in my tracks.

Trixie, Babs, and the gymnastics team—minus Marta, of course—were all there, lined up, waiting for me. Trixie was leaning up against the sinks in her PE gear, her long blond hair back in an obnoxiously high ponytail, her nails long and red, and she was smiling like she had just eaten something delicious. See what I was up against?

"What's this?"

"A frenervention." Trix approached. "Last-time offer."

I couldn't help it, I did an eye roll. "What the heck is a frenervention?"

"It's basically your true friends coming together in a loving environment to tell you what you have to do so that I don't call Roxy," Trix recited perfectly. Her parents were shrinks, remember?

True friends and a loving environment; I couldn't describe it better. "And what is it you want me to do?"

Trix gave me that wide-eyed look. "It's easy, so easy—"

Someone banged on the door. "Hey! I need to pee!"

"Pee somewhere else!" Babs yelled back. "Marta gone. That's it, easy as pie."

Trixie came over, circling. "All you have to do is say nothing, do nothing, that's it." Her cute shoulders bounced like she was saying something sweet instead of kicking a poor girl out of her school because she thought she was better than they were. "Everything we've got planned for you goes away, and you go back to being who you are."

Trouble was—and thank you very much, Mr. Harry Houdini—I wasn't me anymore. I'd stopped being that old me the day I got booted from Malibu Charter and everyone clapped. Or maybe I stopped being me when I met Marta. They were right, no doubt. It would be as easy as pie; it would all go away. And yet.

I looked at my feet in my super cool, beaten-up, hip-hop high-tops and wiggled my toes. Then I looked at their spanking-white shoes, some of which actually had rhinestones. In middle school? Really? Were these the kind of people we should allow to rule the school? "Uh, before I get on board with this and throw Marta to the dogs"—suddenly they seemed so eager, so *happy*—"let me ask you, What has she ever done to you?"

"Um." Babs laughed like it was a done deal. "She stinks like fish."

"Has crap in her hair." Erica shook her head.

Lillian rolled her eyes. "I mean, seriously, you think we can go to the Nationals with *her*?"

TRUE FACT: People don't want others to change. The mean girls wanted Marta to be as hopeless as she could possibly be.

"Well," I said, approaching the situation calmly, "none of that's really true anymore, is it?" I took in their blank faces. "I mean she's changed, right?"

"She's a liar," Trixie said defiantly. "That hasn't changed."

"She's better than anyone on the entire team. Isn't that the real problem?" Their faces fell. "And that she will always be better than you. She's destined for greatness, and you're not. That's the simple truth."

Trixie nodded. "That is one hundred percent true."

I looked at my little nemesis. At least she wasn't totally delusional.

"But it's not gonna matter." Trixie allowed herself a smile. "After Social Services sweeps in and sends her to a home far, far away."

"Nice, Trix, nice." I grabbed my water bottle.

"Nice bottle." Trixie smiled. "You always have that on you, huh?"

"Yep." I unlocked the door and pulled it open. I'd rather run two miles than stay here a second longer with these creeps.

"Hey, Charlie," Trixie called out, "did you really think I'd hold on to your little Malibu Charter secret out of what?" She paused for effect. "The kindness of my heart? Loyalty?" She laughed again. "I called Roxy the first day of school and got the whole scoop. I've known all along."

"Great." I shrugged. "I don't care." Well, I did, but—

"You walk out that door and everyone's gonna know what a total psychopath you are."

The room was quiet. Babs filled it. "You're super pathetic."

The irony of that comment was lost on Babs.

Trix took it all in like she was the queen of the yard. "You talk a good game, you wear all the right stuff like you've got game, but at the end of the day, you're no better than Marta. You'll never have any friends, because you're a loser, Cooper, a total loser, and soon everyone will know the truth."

I turned to look at her. "Yep, they will," I said, and slammed the door behind me. Truth was I could handle the truth getting out. What I couldn't handle was selling Marta out.

The Showdown

Marta and I were out running the laps—she was on her eighth, and I was on my second—when out of the corner of my eye I saw, on the soft, squishy mat of the play structure, Trixie fake a fall to the ground, using the old "I have a ruptured appendix" routine.

"Oh, oh, Coach!" she cried like a Southern belle. "I'm dying, dying!"

I nudged Marta. We slowed to jog in place and watched the whole thing go down. Coach totally bought it, which really irked me, because I'd tried the appendicitis routine like every day, but never, and I mean not once, had he believed me. Trixie's friends swooped in and carried her off the track and into the locker room.

"It's starting." I took a deep breath to ease my nerves, because

240

this time, for the first time in my life, I was not going to stop Trixie from executing her plan.

By the time I had finally run the *entire* mile, everyone had finished. There was just Coach standing over me with his dumb, little stop clock. "Great job, Charlie; you did a thirty-minute mile. That's one for the record books." He laughed. "In fact, I think I see an Olympic coach coming right now."

"You know, sarcasm is *not* a great motivator, Coach," I said, and stormed off to get a drink. "Hey, Marta, you see my water anywhere?"

She pointed to the wall. "You put it right there." Marta looked at her watch. "The cafeteria's about to close, and it's Pizza Monday."

To heck with the bottle, I loved Pizza Monday! "Good point—I'm starving."

So Marta and I ran up to the cafeteria, totally unaware of what they had planned for us, and grabbed lunch. I loaded up on pizza and French fries, all those precious carbs I could have lost during my *mile* run. We took our trays and went outside. Trix and her crowd were nowhere to be seen.

Marta picked at her salad. I'd let her borrow a black top and a pair of my overalls and helped braid her hair. If you didn't know her, you'd think she was normal, except for the panic that surrounded her like a bubble. She looked at her watch again. "Twelve hours and counting." Until her aunt landed. "Permit office tomorrow, and then it will all be okay, right?"

"Right," I repeated, for like the thousandth time that day. I scanned the yard. In the far corner behind the bamboo, I spotted them. Lillian and her crew doing the standard LOOK AT ME I'M SO PRETTY! cartwheels and Trix and Babs looking like the big, fat bosses of the yard, watching it all go down.

After lunch was silent reading time. Mr. L called out, "Find a book, any book!" And then he put his feet on his desk, pulled out his beloved *Huck Finn*, cracked open a bag of nuts, and started chuckling, the poor guy.

I grabbed a book from Mr. L's secret stash of young adult books that he kept on the back shelf. The one I got was about a girl who got her period (gross) and didn't even know what it was because her parents *never* told her about it (demented), and she went *nuts* (funny), and I was really getting into it when something caught my eye. I looked out the window and saw Principal Pickler on his cell walking quickly across the yard like he had a giant pole up his you-know-what.

Mr. L caught me. "Cooper! Read!"

"Fine," I mumbled. Trixie turned and giggled. I was getting that sick feeling.

"Sit!" Marta scolded me. "We don't want to get in any more—"

That's when I saw the nurse—who was so old, she could barely walk—*run* to the cafeteria.

"Charlie!" Mr. Lawson yelled. And I was about to sit when I saw the doors of the kindergarten class open and all the little kids run for their lives toward the lower yard.

I scanned the crowd for Felix, but the kids were running too fast. "What the heck—"

Pickler stopped in the courtyard, hands waving up in the air, hysterical. The nurse came running out. "Principal!" she yelled.

"What?" Pickler yelled back, mad as could be.

"Charlie Cooper!" Mr. L said in a not-so-patient voice. "I said sit down."

"Yes, sir, sorry, sir." I began to sit, but before I did, I saw she had something in her hands—

And then I felt my stomach drop to the floor. "They've got my water bottle."

Pickler stared at it, looked up at me, and ran into the office, the old nurse following him. I fell back on my butt; the room was spinning. Trixie had just gotten me expelled.

Marta looked at me. "Charlie, you're sweating. What's happening?"

"She must have used my bottle to poison the food." I felt like I was in a trance.

Outside, kids were grabbing their bellies, and people were running from the cafeteria to the bathrooms. My brain was spinning out of control.

Trixie turned, put her glossy lips together, and mouthed, *Gotcha.*

I wanted to punch her in the face almost more than I wanted

to run. But their footsteps would be racing up those stairs any minute, and I was so not into being manhandled by Pickler. "I gotta get out of here, Marta."

"What?" Marta lowered her head, whispering. "Now?"

"Yep, right now." I checked to see where Mr. L was, then looked back down on the courtyard. There were more people now, official-looking people, scary-looking people, walking at a brisk pace across the lower yard, meeting in a huddle, and then looking up at my classroom at the same time. I ducked.

Marta got up and looked down into the courtyard. "Oh God!" She covered her mouth with both hands. "They're here!"

I peeked. "Who?"

She pointed. "Social Services."

"What?" I looked down at all the people coming for us.

"See the plastic badges clipped to their belts?" She took a huge breath, tears filling her eyes. "They're gonna take me!" Her face crumpled. "Your parents called!"

"Girls!" Mr. L put down his book. "Is something wrong over there?"

It was now or never. I stood up. "Mr. Lawson?" I took Marta's hand and went to his desk. Everyone in the class stared at us like we were total freaks, which was justified; holding hands at our age was just wrong.

"What?"

I leaned in and whispered the most embarrassing thing I could think of, the only thing that would grant us an immediate

Leave the Classroom Now card, and I had no choice but to play it. It was so gross, it even made me blush to say it. But what could I do? They were coming for us. "Um, sir." I cleared my throat. My head throbbed with shame. "Marta here, well, she just got her, um, period."

He blushed. "Oh, um. Well, I . . ." and started to frantically search for something he did not need.

Marta's face looked like it was on fire.

"I need to take her to the nurse, before it goes all over the—" I paused and pointed to the carpet. "She has stuff." I knew these things because of Pen. She had her own little compartment of what I liked to call *gross* things.

"Fine, fine, *go!*" He looked horrified and waved us out, like he couldn't wait to be rid of us. I knew this too. "Just be quick."

"Sure, yes, absolutely." When we walked out of that room, there wasn't a single eye on a single book. I closed the door tightly behind us; the hallway was empty and so very quiet. I stared down the length of it and was faced with a heck of a choice. Two exits, one on either end of the massive hallway. "Where, which one?" Marta cried, and pulled in *both* directions.

"That one." I pointed to the one farthest from the office, and we ran down that hall so fast, papers flew out of cubbies. I hit the bar on the door, and we ran out, down the outside stairs, until we got to the bottom and hid behind the cubbies.

Marta froze. "Now what?"

I heard voices. We peeked out onto the yard, and Principal Pickler and the badge people in horrible clothes were running up the stairs on the other side of the courtyard, toward our classroom. We had only a minute or two until they got there and found out we'd left, and then all hell would break loose, the school would go into lockdown mode, and they'd call my parents. "We have to get out of here now," I said. "Run, don't stop."

Marta closed her eyes tight, like she was saying a prayer, grabbed my hand, and then we ran across the yard and out to the front of the school. We hit those double doors so hard, I swear I thought you could hear them across the canyon. As we ran down the hill, we looked like escaped convicts, and every driver I looked at seemed to slow down, to stare, to pick up a phone. Or was I imagining it? Were they all calling about us? Turning us in?

We got to the bottom of the hill and stared out at the busy Laurel Canyon traffic and hit the button. The light changed; all traffic stopped and waited for us to cross. Marta pulled me back onto the curb. "It's the first place they'll look," she said. "No way."

I watched the numbers on the crosswalk start their countdown. We had to go; we couldn't afford to miss this light. "Marta," I yelled, "we're not going to the house, all right?" I looked at her fierce eyes. "Trust me, I know a place we'll be safe." I tried to yank her off the curb, but she was stronger than I was. "Come on!"

"We need a day, one day." She looked terrorized.

"I know. I'll get you a day, all right, but you gotta trust me." And she did.

On the Run

We crossed Laurel Canyon and ran up around the house. We stood at the top of the hill, where Mr. Houdini saw everything. Marta was crying, and me, I was waiting for the sound of sirens. They were coming after us hard—that I knew. From here I could see Dad standing, watching eagerly, while the cement truck poured and bricks were being lined up in neat rows. Off to my right, Mom was on her knees, rebuilding the original rock walls. So far no cars with sirens.

When their backs were turned, we ran down to the house and opened the door. I found a cloth bag and tossed it to Marta. "Pack food, a lot of it, because I've got a serious appetite." Meanwhile, I grabbed flashlights and sweaters, and then I remembered the most important thing of all. "Junk food. Mom stashes candy in the third drawer next to the stove. I need candy." I found a piece of paper and started to write.

Marta came over and ripped the pen from my hand. "What do you think you're doing?"

"Leaving a note." I looked at her. "Come on, they'll be worried."

But Marta was firm. "They'll come after us. They'll find a way to get your parents to tell them where we are; they will; they always do. Please, Charlie, once they take me, I'll get lost forever." She took the paper and crumpled it up. "Please, just a day, all I need is a day."

"Okay, fine, one day." I said, feeling not so hot about the idea. "But after one day, no matter what, I'm out, got it?"

Marta took a deep breath. "Okay."

I went over to where the key was hanging and took it. "You ready?" I opened the door, poking my head around the corner. The bulldozers and cement trucks provided awesome cover. Dad was standing over the foundation, his back turned, and the men were all focused on moving the cement around. "Now!" I said, and we ran out into the garden, trying to get to the tunnels, when suddenly the bulldozers stopped. Dad turned.

We threw ourselves behind the giant sycamore tree, our chests heaving, our hearts beating so loudly, it felt like everyone could hear us. The bulldozers started back up again, and we looked around the tree. The workers were pouring again, pouring and spreading. We just had a few more feet to get to the hatch. "Now!" We ran, the key to the new padlock in hand.

I dived on my stomach and slipped the key into the new pad-lock and lifted the hatch. "Come on!" I descended into the total darkness.

But Marta was frozen, crouched over the hatch looking scared and confused. "What is this place?"

"Houdini's secret tunnels." I looked up. "Marta, jeez, come on already, before he sees you!"

Marta climbed down the ladder and grabbed me; she was hysterical. "Oh God, Charlie, I don't like this, not one bit!"

"Stay here." I went back up the ladder, pulled down the hatch quickly. "Calm down, all right?" I opened my bag and searched for the flashlight. "It's here, it's here." And then I found it. I hit the button, and the tunnels were illuminated.

Marta looked around. "Wow! This place is insane!"

We walked down the hall. I shone the light on the horrible pictures of Houdini's mother and wife, the sofas, the human and animal specimens in jars.

"Untouched for eighty years and change."

I took a seat on the sofa next to the skeletons. "Check 'em out."

"What the—" Marta froze, her face draining of color. "They're not rrr-eal," she stuttered. "Tell me they're not real."

"What does it matter?" I put my arm around one of their shoulders. "They're dead. Dad thinks Houdini used them for his magic tricks."

"Can we go now?" Marta couldn't take her eyes off Mr. and Mrs. Bones. "We're so—unprotected here."

"We're belowground, for the love of God, Marta!" I countered.

"Yeah, but if your dad made another key, and he came down here, we'd be trapped," she said matter-of-factly. "Am I right?"

I rolled it over in my mind. "You have a point." And we kept on walking.

But poor Marta kept going on and on about life if she got caught. "They'd never pay for gymnastics. I'd run away—I'd run so far, no one would ever find me. I'd find a gym; I'd hide there, and then I'd practice all night when they closed."

I sometimes forgot that for Marta, gymnastics wasn't just a sport; it was the key to everything. I saw Dad's shovel propped up against the wall and looked at her totally-freaked-out face. "Marta, your aunt is coming. She's on her way, all right? Just calm down."

She took a huge breath and held it until I thought her head might explode. "Okay, Charlie."

"Great." My voice echoed. "Let's go." We walked until we got to the very end of the tunnel, where there was nothing but a huge wall loaded with boulders.

Marta panicked at the sight of it. "If they come, we're done for."

I hit the wall with my shovel, searching. "These tunnels go all the way under Laurel Canyon. If we could just break through, we could go out the other side and spy on 'em!"

"Unless he cemented it all up," Marta, the buzz-kill, said.

But me, I am a glass-half-full kinda gal, remember? I'm not one to give up easily. We middle kids always find a way. I put my hand against the wall. I felt for any crack, my fingers searching for any kind of path, hidden latch, anything. But there was nothing.

After a few hours of searching, Marta just slumped against the wall. "So now what?"

"Oh, I'm gonna keep trying," I announced. I lifted the bag of food from her fingers. I pulled out the food, searched inside, and all I saw was brown bread, cheese, apples, what! I dropped the bag. "You've got to be kidding!"

Marta looked at me. "What?"

"Where's the junk food? The candy? I can't be stuck down here for an entire day without candy!"

Marta winced. "I—I'm sorry, Charlie. I grabbed what I could—"

Now that was it. *Agony!* No sugar! For twenty-four hours! "Crap!" I slammed my fist into the wall, and then all of a sudden, the entire wall moved. I felt myself falling downward, backward. "Marta!"

"Charlie!" Marta reached out and grabbed my hand, and together we fell long and hard into the cold, wet air.

Finding the Magic

You wanna know what I thought about as I fell? My funeral, of course, and how I was gonna look. I just hoped they put my fake glasses on me, a cool Goth black dress, and a pair of rockin' high heels, like my mom's red alligator pumps I've loved my whole life. Maybe with a pair of fishnet tights? Wouldn't that be flippin' fantastic if Mom finally let me wear those?

And then we landed with a splash in what I hoped was some kind of pool and *not* a giant puddle of rat pee. I immediately looked for Marta; she popped up too, thank goodness. "Are we dead?" I hit the button on my flashlight. The pool lit up. *Yes!* The Flashlight Is Waterproof! I loved Dad even more.

"What the—" Marta looked around.

I moved the light against the rocks and water trickled in. "Is this hell?"

"No. Purgatory, maybe." Marta dunked her head again. "Not hell, no, warm pools in hell."

I swam over to the edge and shone the light against the wall I was pretty sure we had fallen from, but there was no opening at all. It seemed like we were trapped underneath. I didn't do well with the whole locked-in thing, and I felt myself beginning to hyperventilate. "How, how are we gonna get out of here?"

Marta took my flashlight and pointed it to a dark corner. "This must be Houdini's secret chamber—look."

I turned, wiped my eyes, and saw it. Against the wall was a giant, brown leather trunk, big enough for a body, *no!* Two bodies. "Oh my *God!*" I felt like I was looking at Jesus himself. "Do you have any idea how long I've been looking for this?" The trunk had big straps and brass buckles. Framed posters of Houdini's circus shows were propped up on the floor behind it. I got out of the water and walked over to the trunk. On top of it was an old brown envelope.

Marta got out too, dripping over my shoulder. "What is it?"

She was getting drops all over my beloved trunk. "Do you mind?" I pushed her away a little while I carefully lifted the flap of the brown paper envelope, which felt like it might dissolve. My heart was racing. I was holding a piece of history, a piece of Houdini. "It's a note." When I read, my voice shook:

If you are reading this, I, the great
Harry Houdini, am dead, and you have
broken into my secret chamber. I have left
behind my beautiful wife

I looked up. "Really? Beautiful? Have you taken a good look at her?"

"Charlie, be nice," Marta said.

"Fine." I kept reading.

and my work. In this box are all my secrets,
the keys to my magic, and the key to
yours. Protect them with your life. Enjoy
life. It is brief.

What! "The keys to all magic!" I could see myself with a wand, waving away Pickler and Trixie, turning Roxy into a rat and Marta into a princess and me, well, me into the chick with the wand that is attached to her hand like Spider-Man's webs are attached to his. I was just about to open the trunk when Buzz-kill grabbed my hand and screamed, "Wait! Should you open it?"

I stared at her like she'd just grown a third eye. "Are you kidding me? Of course I'm gonna open it!" I lifted the hinge, my mind racing with the possibilities. Oh, what will it be? A book of his future tricks? The keys to his past tricks? I could sell this on eBay and make a bloody fortune! I shone the flash-light inside and couldn't believe what I saw.

"It's empty," Marta said softly. "The trunk's empty."

The wood shelves were completely empty, like they'd been wiped clean. "What the—" I stared into the deep, dark trunk. I wanted to cry, I did. "There's nothing in it—man, what a gyp!" Why isn't anything, *anything*, easy, huh?!

"No, wait, there's something." Marta reached in and pulled out the single thing in the trunk. She held it out to me. "A mirror."

I grabbed it, stared at it, took in every inch of it. But it was nothing more than a small silver mirror; it didn't even have jewels or gold, nothing. I felt like smashing it against the wall. "A friggin' mirror! That's it! Who the heck cares about a mirror?"

"The key to my magic and yours." Marta stared into it, summarizing his note. "Protect it with your life—" She closed her eyes. "He's talking about us."

"He's giving us a moral?" I kicked his trunk. "I hate morals, mirrors, life lessons! Jeez, I just wanted some magic, man, that's all I wanted. I *need* magic!"

"But he's right." Marta looked like she'd been kicked in the head. "It's in us. It's up to us."

Clearly it was up to us. It's not like anything ever came easy in this life. All I wanted was a little magic, *or* cash. Now we were back to square one. Suddenly I was tired and starving. I shone the dimming flashlight around. "Where's the food?"

She pointed to the ceiling. "Up there."

"Great, just great!" I wanted to cry. I grabbed my face in my hands. "I'm gonna die, *die*! No food, no way out!"

Marta held the mirror up to my face. "Up to us, remember?"

I tried to slap the mirror out of her hand. "Oh, go away. Just leave me alone to die here, hungry, without sugar!"

Marta walked over to where she thought the rocks had separated and we had come down. "Wait a second. Where was it exactly, the hole?"

My stomach was in a knot; I was so hungry that for a second I thought my tongue was a stick of strawberry bubble gum and I chewed it. "What do you mean, where was it?" I pointed the flashlight to the spot I was 99.9 percent sure we'd fallen from, but there was absolutely no hole whatsoever. "It's gone, Marta, gone." The hole had closed. Forever, sealed.

That's when Marta hauled off and slapped me. Two times. "Stop it with your defeatist attitude!" she yelled. "What's with you? You're the glass-half-full kinda gal, remember?"

"Only when I have sugar," I cried. I could feel myself crumpling into a hellhole of zero sugar. "I have to have sugar!"

She lifted my sagging, depressed chin. "When we get out of here, I'm buying you a month's supply of those candy bears you eat all the time, all right? Just stay with me."

"Really?" Just the thought of those little guys made me smile—red, yellow, green, white, pink. White was my all-time favorite. Pineapple.

"Yes, now get your big butt up and start using that weight of yours to move some rocks." Marta yanked my arm; she was looking pretty mean. "We are going to look for the hole, we are going to sit on every rock until it moves, and believe you me, with the size of your butt, something's gotta move."

"Nice! Criticize me when I'm down." I slapped her back, but I let her pull me up and fill me with that incredible force that Marta had in abundant supply.

The Secret Pin

Three hours—and an incredibly sore butt—later, not a single rock had budged. The flashlight was barely a shadow of light now; how much longer it would last had me seriously worried.

"Houdini, help me!" I screamed. I kicked. "Where is it?" There had to be an escape button; Houdini was the master of escape, right? I turned off the flashlight to save the battery and went back to where I was pretty sure we'd come through the wall. And then—with every bleeding, raw fingertip—I felt like a blind man for cracks, buttons, you name it. Marta walked around the circumference of the pool again and again, kicking rocks, touching seams, screaming as loud as she could, but nothing. On a hunch I grabbed the mirror and rubbed my hands over it. On the back there was a very small but distinct needle. I turned the flashlight on it. "Do you think this could be anything?"

Marta ran over, felt it, and shook her head. "Nah, it's too small—"

But me, I'm the glass-half-full gal, remember? With the last remaining light I went over every inch of the wall where I was convinced we came in. I stopped. "See that?" A tiny, perfect hole in the rock, like it was made for a needle.

Marta rubbed her finger over it and stared at it. "Oh, come on, it's tiny."

"Yeah," I said, "exactly." I took the back of the mirror and stuck the needle into the hole. The rocks separated.

"Oh my God!" Marta covered her face. "You did it; you're a genius!"

Marta led the way up through the rock slide. Just as we reached the top and fell through the other side, the wall closed like an elevator door, *bam!*

I rolled on my cold, wet belly, clutching the mirror to my chest. When we had each finally caught our breath and sat up against the wall, my hunger came back strong. "The food, Marta. Where's the food?"

She handed me the bag and checked her watch. "It's already after eight."

Three and a half hours to go. We put the food out on top of the bag and made sandwiches out of cheese, turkey, and crackers. "Man, for healthy food, this is good!" I devoured everything I could find. And so did she. I checked her watch again. I stared at the walls, listened to the trickle of the springs, checked her watch again. Still only a little after eight. "I have to pee."

"Well, hold it." Marta took a deep breath, holding her knees to her chest.

"For three hours," I mumbled, then decided to listen to my echo. "Hello, hello, hello . . ."

"Stop it!" Marta slapped me. "Where do you think they are?"

"Probably long gone by now." I stretched out my legs, pulled them back in, made the holes on my leggings bigger, took a deep breath, and then made a snow angel in the dirt.

She winced like a mad mom. "What are you doing?"

I had to see just how much trouble I was in. At last count, I was:

1. Being framed for poisoning.
2. Being accused of kidnapping Marta from the laminated card people.
3. Running away.

And that's only the crimes they knew about. I got up and dusted myself off. "Three more hours trapped in here? I can't. I just can't."

She wouldn't move. "I'm scared, Charlie."

"It's okay." I pointed down the dark tunnel. "I know this

place like the back of my hand. I'm just gonna open the hatch, take a quick peek around, and see what's going on."

"No!" Marta clung to me. "You can't leave me! Please!"

"You're gonna be fine, I swear. No way will anyone come down here."

"Fine." Marta looked up at me with her horrible Bambi eyes. "Fine. Just leave me here until my aunt arrives. Then come get me. Okay?"

I resisted the urge to pull her to her feet because, well, part of me knew she was right. It was safer. If she came up and the Social Services people were there, they would take her, *for sure*. "Okay, sit tight, all right. I'll find out what's going on, and I'll be back soon, really soon."

"The mirror, the tunnels"—Marta looked kinda dazed—"don't tell them about them. Whatever you do."

I thought about it for like a second and knew she was right. Houdini had always been there for me. No way would I ever lead the suits to him.

Marta gave me that mean old look of hers. "Promise me."

"Yeah, yeah, I promise," I said. I left her the flashlight but took the mirror—no way was I leaving that thing down here—and I ran down the dark hallway, arms out like a blind person, feeling my way. I found the trapdoor, unlocked it, and lifted it up. My plan was to scurry like a soldier to the house, check in with the parents, and see what was going on. But when the trapdoor opened, there was no need.

"Oh crap!" The entire sky was full of light. A helicopter was circling, its light whipping through the trees, noise filling the air, dirt making it hard to grasp the details until the helicopter light stopped right on my head like I was the target. A loud horn blared. "Stop right there!" I threw my hands above my head and crawled out of the hole like an escaped convict.

A Piece of Me

I walked out into the flashing lights of rescue choppers, hands held over my head, gripping Houdini's mirror like it could get me out of this one, too. The place was surrounded. Police cars, news vans, fire trucks. I felt like I was in a crime scene, and I was the criminal. I saw Mom and Dad, Pen and Felix, all lined up by the front of the house staring at me. I had a sneaking suspicion that I was in *huge* trouble.

"Easy, easy." A super cute fireman on the ground came running toward me. "You okay?"

"Yeah, yeah, I'm fine." I tried to run to Mom and Dad, but the fireman pulled me back.

He yelled over the helicopter, "Is the other girl down there too?"

"Other girl?" I shook my head. "What other girl?" I looked

over at my parents. "Can I just please go now?"

"Where *is* she?" The firefighter put his huge hand on my shoulder.

"How would I know? I was down there by myself doing a little decorating for my party when the door got stuck, that's all. Can I go now?"

"Sure." He nodded, and I ran to my parents. Man, was I happy to see them.

They threw their arms around me. "Charlie!"

Mom whispered in my ear, worried and sad, "Why didn't you tell us about Marta?"

Dad looked just as sad. "We could have helped."

"I promised her I wouldn't." I shrugged a little; I was too tired to shrug a lot. "She was fine. Her neighbor came over to check on her while her aunt was gone, plus Marta doesn't really believe in personal hygiene, so there really wasn't that much to worry about."

They hugged me. "You're a good, good friend."

I looked around at all the chaos. "I didn't mean to worry you."

Dad held my face in his hands. "We knew where you were the whole time, kiddo. The key was gone, and you left this." He held up my beaded turquoise necklace that I put on the hook in the place of the key and kissed me. "Good thinking."

Mom whispered in my ear, "Marta's still in there, right?"

I nodded.

Dad whispered, "Is she okay?"

Out of the corner of my eye, I saw the people running toward me with their laminated badges flashing. Uh-oh. "Mom, Dad, help." They wrapped me in their arms like a protective shield.

"Young lady." The people with the badges came fast. "Where is Marta Urloff?"

"I have no idea." I wasn't gonna take this lying down. That's when mean old Principal Pickler saw me and started marching over, all red.

"Pickler, she's been through hell," Dad said. "Leave her alone."

But Pickler didn't listen. "I wish I could." His eyes were narrow and tired. "Ms. Cooper, we gave you the benefit of the doubt, but you went back to your old tricks, didn't you?" His finger was in my face. "And the lack of originality of it—"

"Exactly," I interrupted.

"Don't interrupt." He held my water bottle and waved it in front of our faces. "There are your fingerprints everywhere. The laxatives used were Romanian, but poor innocent Marta isn't to blame." He took a deep breath and got all puffed up. "You, young lady, are hereby expelled."

Calm as could be, I looked at Pickler. I had nothing to lose anymore. "Think motivation for a sec. Who wants Marta gone most, Pickler?"

"Oh please." Pickler rolled his eyes.

"You have to believe her," Penelope said, getting between

us. "Trixie set up the whole thing because she wanted Marta off the team."

"That girl comes from a family of psychologists! She is well-adjusted; she has been nothing but a pleasure until *you* came along. Whatever she's done, I'm sure you drove her to it." He pointed his finger in my face. "You, Charlie, it's always you."

Felix watched the scene, pulling on Pen's jacket. "Why do they all pick on Charlie so much?"

Mom looked at Pickler. "You should be ashamed of yourself for joining this witch hunt."

"It's called order, Mrs. Cooper; I am restoring order to what was once a peaceful school. Your daughter has brought nothing but chaos and lawlessness to my school. Her lies could have led to horrible danger for that poor child Marta—"

"You don't care about Marta!" I shouted.

"Oh, I care about Marta," he said, glaring. "We never had a lick of trouble with her until your daughter came."

"Charlie didn't hurt her, Principal Pickler," Pen yelled. "She helped her. It was Trixie, Trixie all along."

"What a doofus!" Felix shook his head and went inside.

That's when a policeman came up to Mom. "Ma'am," he said, "where exactly do those tunnels lead?"

"Nowhere; it's a dead end," Dad explained. "It's been walled off." He turned to Pickler. "Don't you at least want to talk to Charlie and Marta to get the whole story?"

"Why, when I have all the proof I need?" He held up my

water bottle. "All the fingerprints, the backstory, the motivation, the character reference?" He hopped over the mud so his dorky dress shoes wouldn't get dirty. "And good luck finding another school for that little troublemaker."

We watched him leave. It felt like it was all over. We were surrounded by all the wrong people: cops, paramedics, and, of course, the Laminated Badge People.

Mom squeezed my shoulder. "Come on, let's go inside, get you warmed up. You're freezing."

"Jerk!" Pen yelled after him. That was when two cops started coming toward us. Man, did they make me nervous.

They looked at Mom, then at me. "We need to talk to your daughter."

"Oh, great." I rolled my eyes. "Look, I didn't do anything, all right. Jeez, you people are seriously barking up the wrong tree!"

They weren't taking no for an answer. "Is there someplace we can talk?"

"Fine, fine." I looked at Mom and Dad. "Let's just get it over with, all right?" But just as we were about to go inside, we heard a loudspeaker blare. "You! Hold it right there!"

We all turned to see Marta, halfway out of the tunnel, waving her hands in the air. "I'm here, I'm here!" Police, firemen, and paramedics rushed to help her, and then the Laminated Badge People caught her in their sights and took off running.

"Marta!" I yelled. "Watch out!" Was she crazy or what? It

would have all been so perfect. All she had to do was stay down there.

I ran over to her. "What are you doing out here?"

"I heard all the noise." She looked at all the mayhem. "I couldn't let you take the blame, Charlie, I couldn't."

I guess that's what real friends are like.

"Thanks, Marta."

Pickler froze. "Marta?" He ran over to her like he was her long-lost dad. "Thank goodness you're all right." Poor Marta had to field a hundred questions and all that unwanted attention. None of this was her fault. It was mine.

Dad was amazed. "Pickler actually seems to care about someone besides himself."

"Yeah, well, he thinks she's gonna bring the team all the way to the Nationals." I'm sorry, I'm an optimistic person, but I also can read humans pretty well, and I knew why Pickler was getting all touchy-feely with Marta, pretending like he cared. Before he knew how great she was, he'd barely looked at her.

"Come on, let's help her," Dad said, and we walked over just in time to intervene.

"You're gonna have to come with us." The Laminated Badge People took Marta by the arm.

"Yeah, yeah, yeah, just don't touch me." Marta shook them off. "Charlie," she called out to me, "come with me, all right, please."

Pickler couldn't believe it. "You want Charlie to go with

you? After all she did?" He was waiting for a response, but everyone just ignored Pickler.

"Mom, Dad, her aunt is arriving at eleven forty-five tonight. You've got to pick her up at LAX—she's on a British Airways flight out of Bucharest. Meet us at whatever jail they're taking us to."

"It's not a jail," declared a humorless Laminated Badge Person. "It's on Wilshire and Third." They wrote the address for my parents. "Follow us down the hill."

I looked around the place; it really did seem like the end of the world, with the giant construction holes, the cops, fire trucks, cars, holes, and ladders, and yet there wasn't a single kid from our school. That hurt, you know? Two girls had gone missing. Two girls had been framed, and yet not a single person had come forward to set the record straight, and that said a lot about the kids I went to school with.

Pen squeezed my shoulder like she knew what I was thinking. "They're not worth it."

"We'll discuss this when your aunt is here." Pickler didn't even look at me; Marta was all he cared about. But Marta didn't care about him. She knew when people were using her. I wondered if she knew that I had used her too, once. Because that was how this whole thing started. I needed to redeem myself. Did I? Was I any better than I was six months ago? I asked myself that as they pushed my head into the car.

"I'll see you guys there." I waved to my parents, and we

started down the driveway. I let my head fall back against the seat and let my eyes fill with tears.

Marta elbowed me. "Charlie."

I bit down hard. "Can I just have a moment?"

"Charlie!" She elbowed me again.

"Marta"—I took a huge breath—"just leave me alone!" I screamed. The driver honked. I opened my eyes and couldn't believe what I saw. A sea of my classmates standing behind the gate with flashlights. The driver honked again. They shone their lights into the car. "Is that our entire class?"

Marta nodded. "Maybe more."

The driver threw the car into Park, rolled down his window, and held up his badge. "Kids, you're obstructing official business."

They chanted, "Charlie! Charlie! Charlie!"

They chanted, "Marta! Marta! Marta!"

Mr. L walked up to our car and tapped on our window. Marta lowered it. "Hey, guys, how are you?" He reached in and held our hands. "I sure am proud of you two girls."

I couldn't believe my ears. "Really?"

"Oh yeah, and now it's time to kick some butt." Looking all tough, Mr. L went over to the driver's side. "Is Mr. Pickler here?" He stood tall, his hands on his hips. "We're looking for Mr. Pickler, and we're not letting you leave until we talk to him."

I couldn't help but smile; Mr. L was so not a tough guy, but the driver went for it. "He's over there," he said. "Make it quick."

"Babs, let's go," Mr. Lawson said.

"What?" I looked at Marta. "Babs? Did I hear that right?"

Marta put her head out in time to catch Mr. Lawson walking Babs and her parents through the crowd toward my house.

I swiveled on the vinyl seat. Marta and I looked at each other, and at almost the same time we put our hands on the handles and jumped out of the car.

"Wait!" The driver turned. "Stop!" He ran after us. But we ran up the hill just in time to hear Babs tell Pickler the truth.

Her eyes were glued to the ground. "Trixie did it all." Her parents nudged her. "All of it. And I helped her. I'm a follower." She turned to her parents, whose faces were about as hard as granite. They nudged her. "And they're making me see a shrink."

"And she's cut off all ties with that Chalice girl." Her mom wiped her wet nose. "I should have known! Kids of shrinks are always bad news."

Pickler's face tightened. "Oh God, don't tell me Cooper's completely innocent."

Babs took a deep breath, nodding like someone who's as guilty as you-know-what. "We crushed the laxatives; we stole her bottle to make it look like what happened at her old school. We framed her."

"But, but why?" Pickler asked, stunned.

"Because she stood up for Marta, and we wanted Marta gone."

He was shaking his head, still not getting it. "But Marta's the team's best chance for winning. What's wrong with you people?"

"But she was Trixie's biggest obstacle," Babs said. "Trixie wanted to be on the team so badly. First she blackmailed Charlie to get her kicked out, and when Charlie refused, she tried to get them both expelled." Babs looked over at the Laminated People. "She called them too."

Pickler took a deep breath and dropped his head. "Where is Trixie?"

"She was right up there." Babs pointed to the hills across the street. "She's been watching the whole thing."

Mom looked at the Laminated People, who were circling like buzzards. She grabbed Marta and hugged her like she was her own kid. "Her aunt is landing tonight at eleven forty-five. Please, she doesn't need you."

"We have to take her," they replied like robots.

"Is *Sixty Minutes* here?" I scanned the place. "Because I swear I want to talk to the people at *Sixty Minutes*. Or CNN, CNN, anyone?"

But there was no *60 Minutes*, dang it. "Dad, can you get my laptop?"

Dad ran inside the house and came back with my computer. He handed it to me, and I quickly pulled up all the documents on Marta's aunt. "Here you go, Dad."

"See?" He pushed the laptop into their faces. "Here they

are, her flight number, her visa. She's Marta's legal guardian; her mother put it in her will." He watched their stern, unbendable faces. "Just let Marta stay with us for two and a half hours, that's it. Then we'll all go to the airport and pick up her aunt."

Marta pleaded. "My aunt and I will be at your office first thing in the morning, and if we're not, you can come get me."

Dad put his arm around Marta. "Don't you think she's been through enough for one day?"

Pen, Felix, and I surrounded Marta—we were an unbreakable chain, but the law is the law, and Social Services wasn't budging.

"Okay, Marta, let's go." I took back the laptop from Dad. "If they have wireless there, I'll show you a good time." I glanced at my watch. "It's only a few hours anyway."

"We'll race over there as soon as we pick her up." Dad kissed us both. "Hang in there."

Marta looked relieved. "It's almost over."

I put my hand on her shoulder. "Yep, soon you'll be home free."

"Hold it!" Pickler called out. "I'm not done with you yet, Cooper."

We turned. Oh, great, I thought, here we go again.

He started walking toward us. "I took one look at you, Charlie, and saw what you were." He shook his head. "The classic middle child, troubled and trouble, but I was wrong about you."

Was I hearing this right? "You were?"

"I was." He put out his hand like he wanted *me* to shake it, after all that he'd done to me. "Yes, I was wrong, and I want to apologize."

Man, I did *not* want to take his hand.

"You did good, Charlie," he said. "Please accept my apology. I made a mistake. We all make them." He glanced at his waiting hand, outstretched and bony. "Even you do."

"That's true, Charlie." Dad gave me one of those nudging looks.

But you know, I didn't really want to forgive him. I wanted to savor the moment, because, let's be honest, when would I ever hear a principal apologize to me again? There was something so delightful about his hand waiting for mine, I just, I just—

"Now, Charlie," Mom cautioned.

"Okay, fine." I looked at all of them. "But I want it in writing, Pick. I want it in those fancy letters, a *huge* apology, and framed, I want it framed."

He nodded. "You got it."

And then I shook his hand super *fast*, because it still kinda grossed me out.

TRUE FACT: Forgiveness is everything.

If I wanted other people to forgive me, then I'd have to forgive them too, right? Plus I was pretty sure I was gonna get a *huge* movie deal out of this one.

Later that night, after we got back from the airport and Social Services, and after Mom and Dad went to bed, I opened my jewelry box and tiptoed down the stairs and out the door. Under the stars I walked up to where my favorite statue in the whole wide world was. The stone was cold. I felt the fake cheekbones and rubbed Houdini's not-so-handsome face. I kissed his forehead, wrapped my beads around his neck, and said a big, fat thank-you. And then I walked back down the hill. But before I got to the house, I looked up to the stars and the sky, and I yelled into the night, "Thanks, Trix, wherever you are."

I hoped she heard me. I knew we were far from over.

Acknowledgments

Phoebe Yeh, my editor, an all-around kind, respectful, and insightful teacher. I am so grateful to have you. Jessica MacLeish, assistant editor, thank you for all the hours spent trying to get Charlie just right. Thank you.

My agents, Victoria Sanders and Bernadette Baker-Baughman, who, from the start, nurtured and protected Charlie like she was their own, promising me they'd find the best home for her, and they did.

My parents—both huge readers, and possibly the kindest most generous people I have ever known—I thank you from the bottom of my heart. Mom, you are a graceful inspiration. Dad, I miss you so much. My husband and my kids—Chiara, Lucia, Pablo, and Rocco—you are the light of my life.

Also wanted to give a huge thanks to Tom Forget and Amy Ryan for the best jacket a girl could ask for. Charlie would be so proud. To a diligent and patient copyeditor, Renée Cafiero, unsung hero: she must hate me and Charlie, but she makes us right. And finally, what is a book without people talking about it and spreading the word? To Lauren Flower, Megan Sugrue, and Olivia deLeon in marketing and publicity for spreading the word from your heart.

Thank you.